Crushed

By

Lynda L. Lock

&

your Friend Sparky

Dedication

In loving memory of my best friend and adventure partner, Lawrie Lock. We crammed a lot of escapades into 39 years of love, laughter, and dancing. Lots of dancing. No regrets.

Lawrie and his next toy – a 1948 MGTC.
Our 1971 DBS-V8 Aston Martin is in the background.

And for my family

We lost three members of our tribe in 2022: my 2nd sister JoAnne Gobert Drayton, my 3rd sister Judith Gobert Bylo, and my eldest cousin William Joseph Gobert.

I wish them happiness in whatever new adventure the universe has planned for them.

Foreword:

The Royal Canadian Mounted Police, RCMP, is the federal force that has policed most of Canada since February 1, 1920, although some Canadian provinces and many of the larger cities now have their own police services.

The Okanagan Valley in British Columbia, Canada, where this story is set, is policed by the RCMP, whose ranks and titles can be a long and cumbersome mouthful of words. For example, the local 'top cop' is responsible for a vast area as the Detachment Commander of Penticton Okanagan Similkameen Regional Detachment. I have shortened the formal ranks to something more manageable where possible.

Since many of my readers are American, I have switched from writing my novels in British English to American English, which creates a challenge with the ranks for the RCMP. Sergeant is the correct spelling for an RCMP officer in Canada, but the common nickname for the rank would be Sarge.

One of the minor characters, Sergeant William Williams, is a Non-Commissioned Officer, NCO. Therefore, he would be addressed as Sarge, or boss, or depending on his relationship with his subordinates, perhaps by his first name. He would not be addressed as sir. That is for commissioned officers, those who receive their commission from the monarch, like the military ranks.

Clear as mud? I hope so.

Cheers,

Lynda

Chapter 1

Highway 5

Alan Fraser's bony, nicotine-stained hands clenched the steering wheel. He rotated his neck, feeling the satisfying crunch as he loosened his tight muscles. The meth was wearing off, and he was losing his edge.

He shouldn't have agreed to this all-nighter, hauling an excavator to a worksite in Surrey and then returning empty to the Okanagan. Late yesterday afternoon Frank, something-unpronounceable, had begged him to take his trip. Frank had a raging fever and was coughing; he could barely stand, much less drive an eighteen-wheeler for another ten hours, and he was willing to pay Alan twice the going rate to keep the customer happy. In Fraser's world, cash was king.

As the Kenworth crested the hill, Fraser stomped the gas pedal and increased his speed, blowing past a slower truck. The posted speed was 110 kilometers, or just under 70 miles an hour, which was nothing for the powerful engine. Equipped with an illegal radar detector, Fraser consistently exceeded the speed limits by a considerable amount.

East of the municipality of Hope, the multi-lane highway climbed higher into the mountains and then descended into Merritt. He took a right turn at the junction of highways 5 and 97-C, then up another steep climb, and he was on the connector, leading into the Okanagan Valley. The high mountain passes created sudden changes in weather, necessitating winter tires from early November to late April. At times the snow was so thick and deep that the truckers were forced to pull over and add cumbersome tire chains.

The heavy-duty wildlife fencing kept most animals off the road, so his biggest challenge was other drivers getting in his way. Year round, the connector was frequently plagued by dense fog at the summit; even so, he trusted his ability to find the road and avoid smashing against the concrete barriers or plowing into a smaller vehicle.

When driving the Coquihalla Highway, changeable weather was always a risk. It could snow anytime, even in August. He had been stuck for hours in traffic jams where the road ahead was littered with passenger cars that had slid off the road, or smashed into each other, or were stuck at the bottom of one of the long steep hills, their tires spinning uselessly on the icy snow.

He hated stupid drivers as well as people in general. It was why he'd scrabbled together enough money to put a down payment on a small, isolated farm.

Just him and a few dumb cows.

Chapter 2

On the Edge Winery Naramata

"So, what do you think?" Mike Lyons asked as he opened the sliding door and stepped outside to a small flagstone terrace overlooking the vineyard. The cool November air flowed inside, a reminder that the nights were getting longer and colder. Mike zipped up his fleece vest.

"It's gorgeous," Jessica Sanderson reached for her jacket, and joining him on the terrace and looped her arm around his waist. Looking over the orderly rows of vines, she could see the shimmer of Okanagan Lake. The first time that Mike had taken her out to the winery, she had fallen in love with the location. It had been summer, and the lavender plants lining the long driveway were blooming vigorously, scenting the warm air with sweet perfume. The scent brought back memories of her travels in France; the delicious food, the interesting people, and the tasty wines.

"It is pretty, isn't it?" Mike agreed.

"Did the Crawfords really offer this to us rent-free?"

"Yep," Mike said. "They wanted to give me a raise for taking on more responsibilities at the winery. I asked if we could live here instead." He hesitated and pulled back a little, "I have an important question to ask you," he said.

Jessica's throat tightened. *Oh god, not that question, not now. I don't know how I'll answer.*

"Will you work in the wine shop? It's the off-season, and we only need someone for a few hours, Thursdays to Sundays."

She sputtered with laughter. "That's your important question?"

"Well yeah." He shrugged nonchalantly. "You don't usually work in the wine shop. Danielle wanted to know if you could help until we shut down for the winter break," he said. "What did you think I was going to ask?" he asked, shooting her a mystified look.

"I'd be happy to help for as long as I'm needed," she said, moving to safer ground by ignoring his second question. "Is it part of the rental deal that I work in the wine shop?" She tipped her head, looking up at him.

"No, not at all. You'll be paid the going rate for whatever hours you work. I just wanted to ask you before I forgot," he said. "You know I get preoccupied and forget stuff."

"Yes, you do," she swallowed a laugh aimed at herself. She'd assumed Mike's important question had been THE question. Instead, she said, "I'm happy to help where I can, and it'll be fantastic to move out of the hotel and into a place that feels more like a home," she turned and studied the cottage. Painted in the neutral hues of the sandy, clay soil and trimmed with soft pine green and white, it was designed to blend into the hillside. The two-bedroom bungalow was equipped with a galley kitchen, a comfortable living-eating area, and, the best part, a wood-burning fireplace for the chilly winter nights. Two full bathrooms would eliminate the morning tango of sharing with Mike. A sly smile slid across her face. She'd challenge him to a game of cribbage to see who claimed the larger en suite and who would walk butt-naked to shower in the guest bathroom.

Mike's wide smile beamed happily at her as he admired the sunlight shining on her long blonde hair. She usually constrained her curls in a single thick plait, but it was loose and beguiling today. He reached for a silky strand and let it slide through his fingers, "I had considered buying a motorhome for us to live in, but the purchase price was crazy expensive, and they depreciate so quickly, it just didn't seem like a good idea."

Jessica's eyes rounded with surprise. This was news to her; however, Mike usually had a dozen or more inventive ideas running around in his head at any given moment. He had probably thought of it, mentally ran the numbers, and decided against the idea all before she had poured her first cup of coffee. "This is far more pleasant than a motorhome," she said. "I've been meaning to ask, how is Dr. Crawford? You haven't mentioned him lately."

"You know you don't have to call him Dr. Crawford; he's fine with just his first name, Keegan."

"Habit. My mom refers to all the doctors at Vancouver General Hospital as Dr. this and Dr. that."

"Keegan seems to have nicely recovered from his heart attack but not from his broken heart," Mike replied.

"A broken heart caused by his swindling daughter, Katherine," Jessica's tone was filled with disdain.

"Drug addiction combined with imminent bankruptcy can make normally rational people do stupid things," Mike countered.

Jessica spun around to see his face, "good grief Mike, you don't honestly believe she isn't responsible for the sequence of events leading to her brother's murder?"

"No, I'm not defending her actions; after all, she wanted Keegan and Danielle to sell their dream winery and bail her out," Mike said.

"Exactly!" She said, gesturing with both hands. "Can you imagine a child so focused on her needs, her wants, that she was willing to collaborate with that Russian mobster, Mikhail Volker, to get what she wanted?"

"Volkov."

"What?"

"His name is Mikhail Volkov. He's the boss. His henchman Ivan Petrov allegedly killed Damien."

Irritated, Jessica flapped her hands. "Whatever their names are, they're evil."

"Yep," Mike said, "and I don't understand evil."

"Me either. I can't imagine the pain the Crawfords are in," she said, then attempting to calm her outburst of indignant anger, she changed the subject. "Anyway, I'm glad you were available to step in as their interim winemaker." She stood on tip-toe, straining to see how far north their view extended. Spectacular! Penticton to Summerland, with Peachland just out of her line of sight, tucked around the bend of the lake.

Mike ran his hand over his nearly bald dome, "funny you mention that. They recently offered me a full-time position."

"Really? Are you going to accept?"

"No, I prefer being a consulting winemaker, my own boss, able to move on when I want. Air travel is possible again, and the world has somewhat stabilized after the COVID-19 shutdown." He lifted one shoulder in a light shrug. "We might want to travel more."

Jessica grimaced and pointed to her aging Mexican mutt. "I love traveling," she made another face.

"I sense a but...coming next."

She nodded, "I'm restricted to traveling in Canada, the U.S., and Mexico as long as Sparky is alive."

Hearing his name, Sparky looked up at her and wagged his stiff white tail. She bent over and vigorously scratched his rump, "Yes, I'm talking about you, pooch."

Sparky had the size and shape of a West Highland terrier, although his head and long black ears were shaped like a spaniel. His wide, fuzzy front feet were larger than his hind feet, and his sense of smell was legendary. He was beginning to show his age, walking a little stiffly and carefully eyeing the height of the sofa before jumping up. The dark mask around his eyes and his fuzzy eyebrows were mixed with gray, blending to white around his muzzle. He was eleven or twelve years old and could live for another five years. In the meantime, Sparky controlled her life in a good way.

"We'll work with it," Mike said pragmatically.

Deciding it was best to veer away from the topic of future adventures, she switched her thoughts. "What about No Regrets in Okanagan

Falls? Are you still going to be their consulting winemaker as well?"

"Absolutely, for now," he nodded. "It's further for me to drive from here to Okanagan Falls. It's manageable because my contract has been cut back from four days a week to just checking in with Chris Berry twice a week," Mike added.

"And Chris is doing okay as the assistant winemaker?"

"Yes, he's got a good head on his shoulders and knows when to ask for my help."

"That winery has been through hell in the last two years. First, Rodney Newcomb murdered the president, Kingsley Quartermain, and then the smoke from the summer wildfires tainted the grapes, making the juice unusable for wine," she huffed. "I'm surprised they are still in business."

"Newcomb allegedly murdered Quartermain," Mike said, "until proven guilty."

"Right. Right. Innocent until proven guilty," she said insincerely, waggling her hand in a gesture picked up from her friends on Isla Mujeres; it meant, more or less, *más o menos*. "His trial is due to start next week, and we haven't been told what day we will be called as witnesses."

"I'd forgotten that we are on the list of prosecution witnesses."

"You would think that since we were at the winery when Ellen Taylor found the body, the prosecutor would advise us the date that he expects us to appear in court."

"I'm not going to worry about it. I'm sure we'll get a letter or phone call soon."

Jessica tipped her chin to meet his gaze. "Have you ever wanted to own a winery?"

"Yep," he chuckled. "Early in my career, I tried to pull together a group of investors."

"And?"

"I realized I wasn't cut out to simultaneously be a farmer, manufacturer, retailer, wholesaler, and marketer."

Jessica scrunched her eyebrows. "What do you mean?"

"As the winemaker, I'm responsible for the wine. I also order bottles, labels, and corks, plus organize shipments for retailers and the BC Liquor Distribution Board. Plus, I oversee the vineyards, harvest, and production. I don't want to be responsible for the tedious liquor control board paperwork, staffing the gift shop and tasting room, or managing the sales reps. I want to make good wines," he said. "Besides, you've heard the popular saying, how do you make a small fortune in the wine industry?"

"You start with a big fortune." Jessica answered with a snort.

"Exactly!"

"When can we move in?"

"Right away."

"Okay, I'll take the car and head back to the Ramada to let them know we're leaving—finally, and pack up our stuff."

"Do you need a hand?"

"Nope, Sparky and I can handle it. You stay here and earn your paycheck. Come on, pooch. We have work to do."

Mike handed her the car keys and leaned in for a kiss. "Do you think you will be back this afternoon with our belongings, or should I assume we are spending one more night at the hotel?"

She checked the time on her phone. "I would rather sleep here. Do I need to buy bedding or dishes?"

"Nope, it's fully furnished. The Crawfords originally planned to do weekly vacation rentals. However, after their lives were turned upside down, neither Danielle nor Keegan wanted to continue with those plans."

Jessica quietly nodded. "I'd better get going. Is it okay if I keep the car for a few hours? I want to stock up on groceries before I return to the winery."

"Take as much time as you need. Call me before you head this way, just in case I think of something I need."

"Will do, bye love, see you soon."

"Love you. Drive safe."

Chapter 3

Naramata Road

Driving south on the east side of Okanagan Lake, Jessica cranked up the volume on New Country 100.7 and accompanied Lee Brice in her notably tuneless voice. *Soul* was currently her favorite tune, and her fingers tapped in time to the infectious beat.

Fall in the Okanagan Valley was beautiful. It was a favorite time for couples to visit the area, sampling beverages and enjoying appetizing meals at one of the Penticton restaurants or at the renowned Naramata Inn. More than forty wineries, eight craft breweries, and two distilleries hosted a swarm of tourists from April to late December. After Christmas, many on-site tasting rooms reduced their retail hours or went into winter hibernation until the end of March.

"We'll do a quick pee stop here, bud, then we have to pack our stuff and leave the hotel," Jessica said to Sparky as she parked the car at Three Mile Beach. Pulling a knitted cap over her head, and gloves on her hands she let Sparky out of the car. They wandered along the road leading to the doggie beach and away from the nudist area, although, in November, she was pretty sure the chance of confronting a bare butt was minimal.

Slowly trailing Sparky while he searched for the perfect place to do his business, she phoned the Ramada Hotel.

"Hi, this is Jessica Sanderson, room 402."

"Good morning Jessica, this is Michaela. How may I help you today?"

"Mike and I have finally found a place to move into, and I'm on the way to collect our things. Could you finalize our bill using the Visa number on file? We'll pay for tonight, too, because of the short notice."

"We're sorry to see you go, but I understand. It will be nice for you to settle into something more permanent," Michaela said. "Don't worry about tonight. We can give you until lunchtime to check out without charge."

"Thank you. I'll be there in about twenty minutes."

"It's no problem. I'll see you soon."

"Thanks, Michaela," Jessica said and disconnected the call.

"Wait, Sparky. I need to pick up your little gift." She ripped a plastic bag from the city's dispenser and resisting the temptation to lick her finger to make it easier; she wrestled it open. "These bags are as frustrating as those flimsy produce bags at the grocery store." She bent and scooped up the still-warm poop. Averting her head, she made a face at the stench of fresh feces and tied the top of the bag. Gingerly holding it with two fingers, she dropped the bag and its odorous contents into the bear-proof garbage can. She quickly checked her hands and decided they were relatively clean and free from the dreaded *cling-ons*, stray bits of dog poop.

"Okay, bud. Let's go pack our things."

Jessica thought about their new home, the beautiful little cottage at On the Edge Winery. She was excited to live in the vineyard with its expansive lake views. A high wire fence encircled the property to prevent the deer from browsing on the vines and grapes. The fence also discouraged packs of coyotes, the occasional cougar, or hungry bears from rampaging through the acreage. Sparky would have room to run if they kept a watchful eye out for ravenous predators.

She lowered the window a few inches and inhaled the chilly air laced with the sweet aroma of over-ripe apples from an adjacent orchard. The delicious smells mingled with the fragrance of sagebrush and pine as the lake shimmered under the diffused November sun. The Okanagan Valley wasn't as colorful as Mexico, yet it had a magnificent beauty.

Although, if she was honest with herself, she missed the vibrancy of Mexico. With country tunes blaring through the radio, she let her memories of life in Mexico wash over her.

Crushed

Mexico was colorful. Isla Mujeres, the Island of Women, where she had lived and worked before returning to Canada, was a tiny sandbar in the Caribbean Sea near Cancún. It was barely above sea level; the highest point was just twenty meters, or sixty-five feet tall. White sand beaches and the quintessential coconut palm trees surrounded brightly painted homes. Red, orange, pink, and purple Bougainvillea flowers clamored over stone walls and draped any supporting structure. Hibiscus. Lilies. Banana trees. Exotic and fragile, the vegetation turned brown in protest if the temperatures dropped below 15C or 60F.

Mexico was loud. Infectious music blaring throughout the night and into the morning was a daily part of life, as were the street vendors calling loudly as they walked from neighborhood to neighborhood hawking their wares. Cheese, handmade furniture, knife sharpening, pottery, freshly squeezed orange juice, Mexican flags for Independence Day in September, or beautiful candy-filled *piñatas* in December and January. Even the propane delivery truck had a musical tune that repeated over and over throughout the day, exhorting customers to bring their empty portable tanks to the street. And fireworks. Fireworks were common for birthdays, particularly the celebration of a young girl's fifteenth birthday her *quinceañera* party. They were also the norm for anniversaries, weddings, local celebrations, national celebrations, or simply because someone had too much to drink and the police chief was nearly a cousin.

Mexico was both ancient and modern. Pyramids built thousands of years ago rubbed shoulders with the relatively newer, 500-year-old influence of the Spanish *conquistadors*. Dinners were long, chatty, late-night affairs that included large extended families. In large business cities like Guadalajara, knowing how to speak Spanish was necessary, and dressing in business attire was the norm, not t-shirts, shorts, and flip-flops. The women wore stylishly beautiful clothing with high heels while negotiating the cobblestone streets or uneven sidewalks. She missed *la vida loca*, the crazy life of Mexico.

She had only known Mike for a few weeks when he asked her to join him at his next job in California. She had readily agreed, knowing Sparky could go with them. Then the pandemic hit, and their plans for California were abruptly canceled. Mike quickly found another contract at No Regrets Winery in the south Okanagan, and they had returned to Canada. In March! The memory of departing from the balmy Caribbean and landing in a late spring snowstorm still gave her the chills.

"The things we do for love." Noticing Sparky's critical side-eyed glance, she said, "don't you laugh at my singing, or you won't get any more steak bits."

He prudently turned his head and looked out the passenger's window.

Chapter 4

Naramata Road

Fraser angrily revved the Kenworth's engine and shouted at the driver of a white Honda Civic. "Move your dumb ass outta my way."

This was his second trip this morning since returning from the all-nighter to Surrey. With zero sleep in the past thirty hours, Fraser fueled his day with pills, cigarettes, and coffee. Another ten minutes and he'd be at his destination, dump the bins, pop a tablet, and head back south for another load, ferrying dozens of high-density plastic containers loaded with grapes from Black Sage Road in Oliver to the Dream Chaser Estate Winery on the Naramata Bench. The annual grape harvest was finished for many of the smaller wineries, although the larger ones, like Dream Chaser, had vast acreages still being picked. The grapes had to be trucked from distant vineyards to the home winery.

One time he'd arrived too early and had to wait, so he'd stood in the vineyard smoking cigarettes and watching while the bins were loaded on his rig. Picking grapes was backbreaking work as far as he could see. It entailed repetitive bending, crouching, and snipping with skinny pruning shears in all types of weather except rain. The winemakers didn't want the grapes picked when wet. The workers snipped the clusters and placed them into plastic buckets, then dumped the full buckets into large bins, which were then moved by tractors to the loading area. Most wineries relied upon a mix of their regular workers and inexperienced enthusiasts. Some wineries marketed the experience as the romance of the wine industry, including a free lunch and a glass or two of wine at the end of the day.

Fraser snorted a laugh. Just give him cash, any day.

He hated this time of the year. The sightseeing, wine-tasting tourists were a pain in his ass, driving slowly and searching for the next narrow driveway that would take them to yet another winery. Still, as an independent contractor, the money made it worth the aggravation.

"I haven't got all day. Move it!" he fruitlessly yelled at the driver, lingering indecisively at the stop sign. Would the idiot choose left toward the city center or right along Naramata Road?

And the jackass chose right, the same direction as Fraser was headed.

As the driver made his turn Fraser caught a glimpse of the man and his passenger. "Figures! Some clueless old farts," he muttered. He sped up and loudly revved the motor again, watching with satisfaction as the driver turned on his right turn signal and nervously edged onto the narrow gravel shoulder to allow Fraser to pass.

"Well, thank Christ for that. He's finally pulling over." Fraser jammed his foot down on the accelerator and sped past the Honda, lifting his right hand in a one-fingered salute. His speedometer touched 90 kilometers per hour as he flashed past the entrance to *La Frenz Winery*. A sudden movement at the side of the road caught his attention.

Deer.

And cyclists.

He wrenched the steering wheel to the left and jammed his foot on the brake. The back end fishtailed in time to his vivid cursing. A woman's scream was cut short as his flatbed slammed into the group, then slowly twisted and toppled over on its side, dragging the entire rig across the pavement until the back wheels rammed into the thick trunk of a tree.

Fraser watched a frightened doe and her two fawns bound up the hill to safety from his inverted position inside the truck. He couldn't see what had happened with the cyclists. "Son of a fricking bitch!"

Chapter 5

Naramata Road

A deafening noise broke into Jessica's daydreams. The corner ahead had a sharp forty-five-degree bend, obscuring her vision for a moment or two. The unnerving sound of air brakes being applied with force. The crunch of metal on metal. A painful scream. And then the ominous rumble of a vehicle grinding across the pavement. Sliding to a smoky stop, a large truck and flatbed trailer lay on its side, blocking the road.

"Oh my god!" Jessica quickly pulled her car to the side of the road and fumbled for her phone with shaking hands. She punched in 9-1-1.

"Police, fire, or ambulance?" A calm, reassuring voice asked.

"All three. There has been an accident on Naramata Road, south of Evans Road, and north of *La Frenz Winery*. It's on that bad corner," she said, momentarily forgetting the emergency medical call takers, EMCTs, who worked in three large centers that covered the entire province weren't necessarily familiar with the local roads. She opened the windows for Sparky and shut off the engine. "Stay here," she quietly instructed him.

Crushed

"How many vehicles?" Asked the woman.

"Only one big truck that I can see, and it is blocking the entire road."

"Police, fire, and ambulance are already on their way," the woman said to reassure Jessica that she wasn't wasting valuable time by asking questions. "How many were injured?" She asked.

"I don't know. I'm walking toward the accident."

"What is your name?" The woman asked. A traffic accident could be highly distressing, and it helped to call someone by their name to talk them through the situation.

"Jessica Sanderson."

"And your phone number, please, Jessica, in case we get disconnected." The EMCT could hear Jessica's agitated breath puffing into the phone as she hurried forward.

Jessica recited the ten digits, then added, "the driver is upside down in the truck, being held by his seatbelts. He's yelling for help, but he looks okay for the moment," she said, then whispered, "oh, my God."

Fraser sniffed; his fuel tank was leaking. He needed to get out of the cab - now. Unlike

Crushed

gasoline, diesel fuel was far less likely to explode; however, it would burn under the right conditions, like a fire in the engine.

His weight strained against the seatbelt mechanism, making unlocking his shoulder harness impossible. Noticing a woman hurrying toward the crash site, he yelled. "Hey, I need help! Get me out of here!"

She was speaking to someone on her cell phone, then suddenly bent over and puked. "Well, you're no damn help," he cursed, yanking hard on the harness. The woman had turned away from him, walking towards something else. "Hey! I need something to cut this damn thing off me," he forcefully yelled.

"Jessica, talk to me," the EMCT urged.

"I see two people and a lot of blood," Jessica replied as she continued walking. Then the call taker heard Jessica loudly retching, "two women, I think," she gasped.

"Jessica, are they conscious?"

"Negative. They are both badly injured, perhaps deceased," she weakly replied, looking at the still bodies and the unnatural angle of the older woman's head. "Wait, I hear a voice, a male. I'm going to see if I can help him," she disconnected.

"Jessica. Jessica." The woman said, then turned to her supervisor, "she hung up."

"Get the Naramata and the Penticton fire and ambulance moving," the supervisor said.

"Already done," a second call taker responded. "I have another call that is related to your incident. A truck driver was speeding when he passed this caller and his wife. They are on the Penticton side of the crash and can't see anything except the truck blocking both lanes."

"Are they able to check for survivors?"

"Negative. The gentleman said they are both elderly and not stable on their feet."

"Okay, ask them to remain in their car until an officer can get their statement," the supervisor replied. "Marnie, try to reconnect with your caller for an update. I'll contact the RCMP superintendent. They can coordinate with the city for re-routing traffic. This is going to be a long one."

Jessica's chest tightened and she concentrated on slowing her breathing. "You can do this. You've dealt with serious injuries before." Her mom, Anne Sanderson, was a trauma nurse, and her dad and brothers were firefighters. Family mealtime conversations could sometimes be graphic and filled with dark humor, a coping mechanism for many emergency personnel who dealt with death and illness daily.

Pulling off her gloves she pressed her fingers to the first woman's neck, searching for a pulse. Nothing. She bent lower to listen for breathing, watching to see if her chest was moving. Still nothing. She gently felt under the woman's head; a sharp bone splinter jutted against her fingers. The battered face, visible under the knitted cap, was vaguely familiar, although Jessica didn't have time to determine if she knew the woman. She was likely deceased, and there were three more people to assess.

She shouted to the male. "Where are you?"

"Down here, in the ditch," came his ragged reply.

"Are you bleeding?"

"Lots of scrapes and cuts, and I think my leg is broken," he responded, his voice raspy with pain. "I'm okay, but what about my mom and sister? Are they okay?"

"If you're fine for a few more minutes, I will check on them first." She replied, dodging his question. ABC, airway, breathing, circulation. If he was talking, his airway was clear, and he was breathing. If he hadn't noticed any substantial bleeding, he'd be okay for a few more minutes. Shock would be her next concern for the man.

"I'll be fine."

"What's your name?"

"Tyler. My mom is Lorna, and my sister is Camden."

Jessica bent over, putting her hands on her knees she inhaled deeply and exhaled slowly. That's why the woman looked familiar; she knew this family. The Sinclairs. Her hands trembled. She straightened, forcing her voice to sound confident, "Tyler, this is Jessica. I know your parents. We've met before. Are you sure you are okay for a few more minutes?" She listened intently.

"Yes," he replied, "look after my mom and sister."

A shaky male voice said, "I called 9-1-1."

She turned, noticing a thin, white-faced man standing behind her, "thank you, I did too. Can you evaluate the truck driver? I'm going to see about the young woman."

"I think both of those people dead," he shouted, as he pointed at the women.

Jessica gestured sharply with her hands. "Shhh, the son is nearby and might hear you."

"Should I check him first?" He ran a hand over his pale face, nervously wiping sweat from his forehead.

Jessica assessed her new helper, wondering if he would faint and become the fifth person she'd have to assist, "are you going to be okay?"

"Yes, yes. I'm fine. Just not used to seeing so much blood."

"If you are absolutely sure you'll be okay, check the truck driver first and then the young man. His name is Tyler, and he's over there." She pointed toward the ditch. "He thinks his leg is broken, so don't move him."

"I'll be fine." Still wiping sweat from his face, he started walking toward the immobilized truck.

Jessica watched him momentarily, then turned her attention back to Camden. Stepping carefully to avoid the spreading pool of blood, Jessica squatted beside the teenager who was face down on the side of the road. She wrapped her fingers around the girl's wrist. A faint and irregular pulse. She searched for the carotid pulse in Camden's neck. The same fluttery beat. Her breathing was labored and infrequent.

"Camden? Can you hear me?" She unzipped her warm jacket and gently spread it across the girl's back, hoping to help in some small way. So much blood was seeping from the young woman's mouth that she didn't dare turn her over to assess her injuries. The blood might block her airway, or the movement could disrupt her heart's erratic rhythm. Her phone rang. She noticed she'd missed another call from the same number. "Yes?" she snapped. Her fingers again felt the vein on Camden's neck, weaker still.

"This is Marnie, the emergency medical call taker. Is this Jessica Sanderson?"

"This is Jessica," she answered, as shivers rattled her teeth. Anxiety. Adrenaline. And cold.

"Two ambulances will be there within minutes. Can you update me?"

"Lorna Sinclair," she lowered her voice, "possibly deceased. Camden Sinclair, critical," she continued speaking in short bursts of information. "Tyler Sinclair is talking to me. I haven't gotten to him yet. He thinks he has a broken leg. The truck driver appears conscious. I don't know his status. Another person is with him now."

"Do you know the family, Jessica?"

"Yes, I do."

Marnie locked eyes with her supervisor, who was again listening to the exchange with a second headset, "You're doing great, Jessica. Just a few more minutes, and you'll have lots of help."

"The injured are all on the north side of the accident. The first-responders will have to find a route around the truck," Jessica replied, "and I smell diesel fuel."

"Understood," Marnie answered, swiftly typing that information into the computer. Put me on speaker, and please stay on the line."

"Okay," Jessica complied, then turned her full attention to the young woman, "Camden, help is coming. Stay with me. Your brother Tyler needs you." She gently held her hand as her pulse fluttered irregularly. "Can you hear the sirens, Camden? Help is here. Stay with me."

Within minutes a firm hand touched her shoulder. "We've got her now. Thanks."

She mutely nodded, pushing herself to stand and move away. Hot tears coursed down her cheeks. She swayed on her feet and was surprised when her ass hit the ground.

"Jessica, are you okay?"

"Just a little dizzy." Jessica squinted up at Cst. Evan Swan. "When did you get here, Evan?"

"Just now." Swan squatted beside her. "I always knew you were a little dizzy," he whispered with a half grin.

Her head drooped, and fresh tears wet her face.

"I'm sorry, Jess, that was stupid," he said.

"I'm crying for the Sinclair family. Not me."

He nodded sadly. "Believe me, I know exactly how you feel. Come on, let me help you up. We'll get someone to check you over."

"No, the ambulance crew has more important things to do," she said, reaching for his arm. "Just get me to my car. I'll rest there for a few minutes."

Swan pulled her to her feet and wrapped a supportive arm around her shoulders.

Her eyes followed the actions of the ambulance crew as they placed Camden on the stretcher and prepared to transport her to the hospital. "I hope she makes it," she said.

Swan said nothing as he walked Jessica back to her car. He'd seen the pool of blood on the pavement.

Chapter 6

Naramata Road

Cpl. Caitlin Smith, General Investigative Section of the Penticton RCMP, was an amateur wine geek. The grape harvest was her favorite time of the year, except today the dazzling morning was ruined by the sharp odors of diesel fuel, hot metal, shredded rubber, bodily fluids, and blood. She pulled a warm cap over her head and strode toward Cst. Swan.

"What have we got, Evan?" she asked.

Bundled in his heavy jacket, Cst. Swan stood in the middle of the road. His cruiser blocked any attempts from drivers hoping for a route around the crash site. Other uniformed officers redirected both northbound and southbound traffic away from the scene. Nothing—vehicles, pedestrians, or cyclists—would pass through for quite some time.

Caitlin swiveled her head left and right, surveying the destruction. The disabled trailer lay across both lanes, north of the entrance to *La Frenz Winery*. Large plastic bins of grapes had spilled their precious cargo across the road and into the ditch. As Caitlin's right foot slipped on the slick layer of crushed berries and fuel covering the roadway, she pinwheeled her arms, struggling to regain her balance. Swan clamped his hand on her bicep, steadying her.

"Sorry, I should have warned you," he said. "Come with me," he said and walked toward the vehicle. "We need to go around this way. Be careful of your footing."

Caitlin followed Swan as he led the way around the front of the vehicle to the other side. On the eastern edge of the roadway, a mound was covered by a heavy tarp.

"That truck struck three cyclists." He pointed at the distorted wreckage of bicycles, one red and two blue, that lay where the riders had been mown down. Nothing could be moved until the FIS, the Forensic Investigation Section of the RCMP, had documented and photographed the scene, and the coroner gave the okay to remove the body. "The mother, Lorna Sinclair, is deceased," he pointed to the bundle lying in front of a mangled bicycle. Swan's voice faltered, "her teenage daughter, Camden, is on the way to the hospital, but it doesn't look good."

"Two in one family. That's awful." Caitlin huffed out a sigh.

"Three," he corrected, "the son, Tyler Sinclair, has a broken femur and has been transported to Penticton Regional Hospital. He knows his mom died, and his sister is badly injured. He's emotionally in rough shape."

"I can't imagine what that poor kid is going through," she said. "Could he give you any details?"

"From the little information I could get from him, they were cycling single file on the edge of the road when the deer startled them. Tyler said he heard a loud grinding noise like the brakes on a big truck." Swan swallowed and briefly looked away. "He doesn't remember anything else."

"Do you know if Tyler's father lives in Penticton and if he's been notified?"

Swan frowned. "I haven't had time to find out."

"I'll arrange that with Sarge," she wrote a note in her book. "What about the driver?"

"He has also been transported to the hospital in a separate ambulance."

"Did he give you any information?"

"Only what I got from his driver's license. Alan Richard Fraser. Date of birth 91-10-24. 183 centimeters, six feet tall. Brown hair. Brown eyes. Caucasian," Swan recited. "He refused to talk about the accident. Kept saying he was in too much pain to think clearly." Swan swiped at his phone, showing Caitlin a photo of a thin-faced man staring into the camera for the official driver's license photo. His lank hair reached his shoulders and rested on a red plaid shirt. She couldn't see his hands, but judging by the indent in his hair just above his ears, she was sure that he'd just removed his baseball cap when the photo was taken.

Smith raised an eyebrow. "Do you believe him?"

"It's hard to tell. I didn't see any broken bones. There could be internal injuries, but the airbag was deployed properly. He spent a few minutes inverted, held by his seatbelt. I imagine that was not a comfortable way to be trapped."

"Alcohol?"

"I didn't smell anything. However, I suspect drugs. I've asked the hospital to test for drugs and alcohol."

"Good," Smith said as she swept her gaze over the accident site, "with a fatality, it will take some time to clear the scene. We need to direct the traffic to a bypass route."

"There isn't one." Swan gestured with his arm, "on this stretch of Naramata Road, there is no alternate route."

"Nothing?" she asked, incredulous that the eastern side of the community was serviced by only one road.

He slowly shook his head. "Nope. Sarge contacted the city. There is no alternate route."

"That complicates things—in a big way."

"Yes, ma'am."

Attending a fatality was difficult, plus there was the uncertain status of the teenage daughter. Swan was stressed; she could hear it in his abrupt response. She softened her expression. "Good work, Evan. I'll leave you to it."

"One more thing, Caitlin," Swan said.

"Yes?"

"Jessica Sanderson was the first on the scene and knows the victims. She is sitting in her car—over there," he said, a knowing smile pulled at one corner of his mouth as he pointed to a car that Caitlin recognized. "She has her dog Sparky with her."

"Great," Caitlin muttered, glaring at the car, "just what I need." To Caitlin's annoyance, Jessica was a well-known meddler who had indirectly assisted with two previous murder cases. She also happened to be a close friend. "I'll call Sarge first to arrange a notification for the family, then deal with Jessica." She dialed their boss's number.

Sergeant Williams gruffly answered, "yes."

"Sarge, I'm attending the fatal accident on Naramata Road. We need an immediate next of kin notification for Lorna Sinclair, and the family should be told that the two teenagers are being transported to the hospital with injuries. The daughter Camden Sinclair is critically injured. Her son Tyler Sinclair has a broken femur."

"Do we have a name for the next of kin?"

Caitlin looked over at Jessica's car, "one minute Sarge. I think I can get that information for you. I'll call you right back."

Perched on the console between the two front seats, Sparky spotted Caitlin walking toward the car and wagged his tail in greeting. Jessica appeared to be sleeping. Her eyes closed, and her head tipped back against the headrest; her face was pale and drawn.

"Jess? It's Caitlin," she said tapping lightly on the closed window.

Jessica's eyes flew open, and she powered down her window. "Sorry, I must have drifted off." She straightened in the seat and reached to open the door. "I'll get out. Sparky might need a pee."

"Okay. Keep him on his leash, please."

"I know. Evan has already reminded me that he didn't want Sparky contaminating the evidence." She snapped the leash to his collar, then opened the door. Swinging her feet to the pavement, she braced one hand on the doorframe to stand.

"Are you injured?" Caitlin said, scrutinizing Jessica as she cautiously stood up.

"No, I made a fool of myself by falling flat on my ass a few minutes ago. Evan helped me to my car."

"You're shivering."

"I'll be fine. Come on, Sparky, have a pee," she said, walking him to the grassy verge.

"Do you feel up to answering a few questions?"

Jessica's stomach clenched at the thought. "Sure," she half-heartedly answered. Desperate for a drink of water and a nap, she wrapped her arms across her chest trying to keep warm.

"Do you know the name of Lorna Sinclair's husband and presumably the father of her children?"

"James Sinclair, from Summerland. They own a vineyard, but I don't know the phone number or address."

"Thank you. I need to update my boss. I'll be back in a minute."

Caitlin hit redial and walked a few feet away from Jessica. "Hi, Sarge. Next of kin is James Sinclair in Summerland. No other information," she said. "Thank you, Sarge," she replied to his assurances that he'd make sure the Summerland RCMP immediately handled the next of kin notification. Rejoining Jessica, Caitlin asked, "is it okay with you if I use my phone to record our conversation instead of trying to write while walking?"

"That's fine, but what time is it?" Jessica felt muzzy-headed, as if she had woken suddenly from a stressful nightmare.

"It's almost noon."

"Oh hell, I was on the way two hours ago to remove our things from the Ramada. Give me five minutes to call Mike and explain. Then he can call them," she reached back inside the car, grabbed her phone from the cupholder, and called Mike.

Caitlin pointed at her phone, "okay to record?" she asked.

Confused, Jessica hesitantly nodded in agreement as she told Mike what had happened. "I'm fine, honey," she insincerely assured him. "I just need to speak with Caitlin for a few minutes, and then I'll come home. Please let the hotel know we've had an unavoidable delay. I'll deal with it tomorrow. Love you too. Bye."

"I thought it would save time if I recorded you explaining to Mike what had happened."

"Sure, that's fine." She reached inside the car and placed her phone on the dashboard. Acutely thirsty, she checked the door pocket, searching for the open water bottle she kept there for Sparky. "What else do you need to know?" She tipped the bottle, drank the lukewarm contents, replaced the cap, and flipped the empty bottle back into the car.

"Did you witness the accident?"

Jessica dropped her gaze, mentally visualizing what she had witnessed. "Did I? I don't think so." Sparky tugged lightly on his leash, he wanted to investigate another bit of vegetation, so she followed him. "That's a sharp corner, so my visibility was limited until I got closer. I remember the horrific noise. I didn't know what was making the noise until I saw the truck sliding across the pavement, and then it suddenly stopped as if it was caught on something."

"The rear end hit a large tree," Caitlin confirmed. "Okay, that's enough for now. Will you come to the station tomorrow morning so that I can take a proper statement?"

"Do you think Sgt. Williams will let me through the door? Didn't he say I may not be on his Most Wanted poster, but I am at the top of his *Unwanted* list?"

Caitlin smiled briefly. After what Jessica had experienced, it was good to see a flash of her sharp wit.

Chapter 7

On the Edge Winery

Emotionally and physically exhausted, Jessica sat in the car on the gravel drive in front of the cottage. The heater blasted out hot air as she tried to warm her shaking body. Ending her phone call to Caitlin, she rested her forehead on the steering wheel. Camden had died on the way to the hospital. Unwanted images flickered behind her eyelids—such a tragic day.

It was the first time she'd seen the catastrophic destruction caused by a large vehicle hitting cyclists, but not her first time dealing with traumatic injuries. Three years before, her mother's younger sister, Pattie Packard, had been shot at Carlos and Yasmin's wedding on Isla Mujeres. The gunman, a lieutenant for a Cancún drug lord, had been aiming for Jessica. His boss was livid that Jessica and her close-knit group of friends had temporarily disrupted his drug business on Isla Mujeres. At the last moment, her auntie had leaned forward to speak to Jessica and unwittingly moved into the bullet's path.

Anne Sanderson, Jessica's mother, had also been a guest at the wedding along with the rest of the Sanderson clan. Anne had stabilized her sister's pneumothorax, the hole in her chest that prevented her lung from properly inflating, until Dr. Marion arrived from her nearby home. Pattie, the Sandersons, the bride and groom, and Dr. Marion boarded Diego's charter boat and set off for the hospital in Cancún.

Unlike Lorna and Camden Sinclair, Pattie survived.

Sparky woofed once, and Jessica looked to see what was happening. Mike was walking toward the car; she opened the driver's door and wearily put her feet on the driveway. Sparky pushed past her legs and immediately scurried to the nearest bush.

"I heard the tires crunching on the gravel a few minutes ago and got worried when you didn't come in." He said, searching her face. "How are you doing, honey?" He pulled her into a comforting hug, resting his chin on her head.

"Surviving," she flatly answered. Encircling his waist with both arms, she leaned her face against his chest and breathed in his familiar scent.

"Come inside," he shifted his position and wrapped an arm around her shoulders, "I'll make you a nice cup of tea with sugar," he said, leading her toward the cottage with Sparky at their heels.

"That's very British of you, my love. Hot tea with sugar for a person who has had a shock or has received tragic news," she said as she tossed her keys on the hall table and kicked off her shoes. "Right now, I'd prefer a stiff whiskey over ice."

"Done. Put your feet up in the living room."

"I'll be in the bathtub. I'm freezing."

"Weren't you wearing a jacket?"

Her eyes filled with tears, "I used it to cover Camden," she whispered. "I was hoping to keep her warm."

Mike pulled her close. "You start your bath." He kissed the top of her head and released her. "I'll just be a minute with your whiskey."

Jessica turned on the taps and stripped, dropping her clothes in an untidy heap on the floor. She stuck a toe in the water, adjusted the temperature, and slowly lowered herself into the hot water. Sparky settled on her discarded clothing, his soulful brown eyes intently watching her. "Silly dog, I've told you before there isn't a secret escape route from the bathroom. I'm not going anywhere."

He gently tapped his tail on the tile floor and stayed put. Guarding her.

"Isn't this cozy? The whole family is here." Mike handed her a drink and set his on the counter. He closed the toilet lid and perched beside her. "Would you like to talk about it?"

"Umm. It's harder to deal with because we know the Sinclairs and even more difficult because

I couldn't do anything to help." Shoulders sagging, she tilted her chin up to look at Mike, "When I got home I phoned Caitlin from my car. Camden didn't survive. That's not public knowledge until the family has been notified, and I promised we wouldn't say anything." She cupped her hands and washed the tears from her face. "I had to know."

"Ah shit, that's awful. I'm so sorry, Jess."

"Half of the family, gone." She splashed more water on her face. "How does a family survive a double tragedy? Grandparents or elderly parents dying, that's the expected order of life, but a daughter and a mother on the same day. Unthinkable." She reached for the glass and gratefully sipped the peaty liquid.

"It is going to be rough for James and Tyler to get through the next few months or even years," Mike agreed. "My one-hundred-year-old friend Edie Parker says you don't get to choose the day you're born, and you don't get to choose the day you die," he said. "I agree with her. Life is what you make it, but you don't have control over how long you will live."

"She sounds like a wise lady," Jessica said.

"She's pragmatic about life," he said, "and death."

"Do you know if the Crawfords are close friends of the Sinclairs?"

"We buy grapes from Sinclair Vineyards, and they've been to the same wine-related events at one time or another," he exhaled loudly. "The accident and road closure has been on the news. No names were given until the other family members have been notified. I'll pop over to the main house and see if they know about Lorna and Camden."

"What about Keegan?" she asked. "I mean because of his recent heart attack."

"Good point. I'll check with Danielle first. She can decide about telling Keegan," Mike replied, "although he's bound to find out, one way or the other. The wine industry is a tight, close-knit community."

"True," she agreed. "Where is the Sinclairs' vineyard? I don't remember if you mentioned it before."

"It's on Morrison Drive, in Summerland. It's not a big vineyard, but they grow good grapes, and we buy everything."

Jessica inhaled another mouthful of the malt whiskey and slid lower in the tub until her chin touched the hot water. "In case I haven't told you today, I love you very much, Mike Lyons."

"And I adore you, Jessica Sanderson."

Chapter 8

Naramata

"Nathan?" Carrying full coffee cups in both hands, Heather Lapointe walked from the house to her husband's workshop. She used her elbow to push down on the door handle and shoved the door open with her hip, "I've made a fresh pot of coffee, honey. You've been at this since dawn, and I thought you could take a break."

Silence greeted her.

"Nate?" She walked to his workbench and set the cups down, taking care not to spill the liquid, "where are you?" She scanned the workshop, noticing his recent project was on the lathe. "Honey?" She opened the entrance door and walked a few steps to double-check that their vehicles were still in the driveway, then mumbling to herself, she retraced her steps. "Both cars are still here, so he hasn't gone to the hardware store or the lumber yard."

Heather pulled her cell phone out of her pocket and punched in Nathan's number. His distinctive ringtone responded from behind his toolbox on the workbench. She ended the call, tapped the edge of her phone in the palm of her hand, then tucked it back in her pocket.

Maybe, he's in the garage? She opened the workshop door again and angled her steps toward their two-car garage. The garage was so crammed with Nathan's projects and supplies that both vehicles had to be parked outside, no matter the weather. It annoyed her to hell and back, but it wasn't worth the arguments to get him to pare down the mound of 'his good stuff,' as he called it. Entering via the side door, she shivered as she stepped inside and instinctively reached to turn on the lights but stopped when she realized they were already on.

"Nate? Are you in here?"

A strangled moan escaped from behind the pile of furniture that he'd made in preparation for the upcoming Christmas craft fairs.

"Honey! What's happened?" She rushed toward his voice.

His eyes bobbled from side to side as he frantically tried to speak, but his voice was soft and garbled. He jerked a few times as if he was trying to sit up. Drool escaped from the left side of his mouth.

With one hand on his chest, Heather gently held him down, "no, stay there, sweetie, while I get help." She pulled her phone from her back pocket and dialed 911, willing the phone to be answered quickly.

"Police, fire, or ambulance?"

"Ambulance."

A few seconds later, "Ambulance services, what is your emergency?"

"My husband, Nathan. Something is wrong. He's lying on our garage floor and can't speak properly."

"What is your location?" The call taker asked, "and your phone number."

She recited their address and phone number, adding, "we're in our garage."

"How old is your husband?"

"He's still young. He's only fifty-five," Heather replied. *He is young. But what's happening to him?*

"And what is his name?"

"Nathan Lapointe."

"I have already dispatched an ambulance from our Naramata station, ma'am, and I'm communicating with them. In the meantime, I will ask you a few more questions."

"Okay."

"Is one side of his face slack or drooping?"

She studied his face. "Yes," she replied, "the left side." A chill swept through her. *Why was it lopsided?*

"Can he lift both arms?"

"I don't know, he's lying on our garage floor," she repeated.

"Ask him to move his arms a little, like he is making a snow angel."

Perplexed, Heather told her husband, "Nate, honey, she wants you to move your arms like you are making a snow angel."

Nathan struggled with her request, finally moving his left arm forty-five degrees from his body.

"Can you move your right arm, sweetie?" Staring at his inert right arm, her heart thudded in her chest.

His frightened eyes juddered to the right, trying to see if his arm was moving.

"Don't worry, honey." She patted his shoulder in what she hoped was a reassuring gesture, then spoke to the call taker. "His left arm moves, but not the right."

"The ambulance will be there in a few minutes. Do you have a blanket to keep him warm?"

Heather glanced at the bewildering mound of stuff in the garage, but of course, there weren't any blankets, at least not that she could see. "I'll run into the house and get one."

"Don't run. We don't want you injured as well. Walk quickly but carefully and stay on the phone with me."

"Okay," she smiled timorously at Nathan. "Honey, I'll be right back. I'm just going to get a blanket for you. It's so cold here in the garage." His garbled reply made her scurry away, swiping the tears from her face. She was terrified that he would see her fear.

As Heather exited the house, awkwardly balancing two blankets and her cell phone, she could hear the siren approaching their street, "I hear the ambulance," she said.

"Good. Put a blanket over your husband. That will help keep him warm until they arrive."

Heather gently spread one blanket, then the other, over Nathan as he vibrated with shivers. "Help is coming. You're going to be just fine, my love." She bent and gently kissed his cheek. "Just fine."

The siren's wail abruptly ceased as the vehicle thundered into their driveway, lights flashing. Heather ran outside, waving her arms overhead. "We're in here!" She shouted as the driver stepped out.

The attendants quickly retrieved the stretcher from the van and hustled toward her. "Where is your husband?"

"Inside on the floor." She ran toward the garage, pointing at Nathan.

With one glance, the second attendant knew they had to get their patient to the hospital as fast as possible. "Mrs. Lapointe, please get your husband's medical card and any prescriptions he takes. We'll transport him immediately."

"His wallet is usually in his back pocket," she said, then rushed inside the house, snatching up her purse, his blood pressure medications, and her jacket. Then she added his jacket to the pile. Maybe this was a false alarm. He'd need his jacket for the ride home.

Chapter 9

Naramata Road

"Is there a route around it?" The driver asked their dispatcher via the handsfree. Heather noted her name tag: Rebecca.

"No. The police and the municipal workers have been trying to find a road that connects from one side of the accident to the other, but with no luck."

"So, what do we do?" Rebecca spun the wheel, steering the ambulance onto the main road. She'd have to activate the siren soon but needed more information before the deafening cadence made conversation difficult.

"Pull up to the barricade, unload, walk the stretcher towards the southern side of the accident, and swap stretchers with the Penticton unit, then return to your station. They will transport the rest of the way to the hospital."

"Are the RCMP expecting us?"

"Yes. They have been advised of the situation and will facilitate your transit through the accident scene."

"Do you know if there is a traffic backup in the area?"

"One moment."

"What's happening?" Heather whispered.

The woman raised a finger in a wait-a-moment gesture, listening for the answer to her question.

"This is dispatch. The on-scene officer says many vehicles are arriving at the barricade and being turned back, so be advised you could encounter heavy traffic in both directions."

Rebecca sucked in a breath. Annoyed drivers could be as unpredictable as panicky drivers in their response to the wail of a siren. "Copy. We're ten minutes out. Will the other unit be on the scene when we arrive?"

"They're on the way."

"Roger, out." Rebecca disconnected and spoke loudly enough for her partner, who was attending Nathan Lapointe, to hear her. "David, we have a slight glitch. There's been a traffic accident between Red Rooster and La Frenz on that sharp corner. The road is completely blocked. We must walk Mr. Lapointe and the stretcher through and hand him over to the unit coming from Penticton."

"Copy that," David answered calmly. Neither Rebecca nor David wanted the Lapointes to panic. Still, a delay of a few minutes while walking the stretcher around the disabled vehicle could make a massive difference to his chances of a successful recovery.

"Walk his stretcher? Isn't there another route?" Heather cried.

"Not according to our dispatcher," Rebecca answered evenly.

"There are dozens of roads branching off the main road. Surely some of those connect?" she asked.

"I'm sorry, Mrs. Lapointe. The city workers and the police officers have been searching for an alternative route. There isn't one."

"But, Nathan," she whispered.

"I know, ma'am. We'll do everything we can to ensure he is well taken care of," Rebecca answered. She didn't say that a delay, any delay, in getting a stroke victim to advanced medical care was disastrous. As she accelerated the vehicle, she reached for a dashboard switch, and the ear-splitting wail commenced. She pointed at the ear protectors that she had given Heather. "Put those on."

Heather numbly complied, then clung to the grab handle above the door, hanging on as the bulky van thundered along the winding highway. If she twisted and looked over her left shoulder, she could see Nathan lying on the stretcher with an oxygen mask on his face. David reached forward, rechecking his condition.

Before the vehicle had started to move, David had inserted an IV line. He explained that Nathan was most likely suffering from a stroke and that the blood thinner should help prevent further damage.

Stroke. That word sent shivers of fear through her body, and her teeth rattled against each other. She hugged herself, trying to control her shaking.

"You're feeling the effects of the adrenaline," Rebecca explained kindly. "Fear can make you feel shaky and cold. This should help a bit." She increased the temperature a couple of degrees.

Unable to speak, Heather nodded once, letting her know she had heard.

The boundary sign between Naramata and Penticton flashed past, then a montage of winery names in rapid succession, and suddenly a line of traffic appeared. Rebecca slowed and activated a secondary tone, telling drivers to move over. Now! The southbound cars inched to the right, closer to the drop-off, and the northbound vehicles huddled against the dirt bank. Two drivers froze in place, unable to move either left or right. Twisting the steering wheel, Rebecca kept the bulky van moving, slaloming like an experienced skier through the winding course of the vehicles impeding her route.

Heather's breath caught in her throat. Nathan's treatment would be further delayed if any driver panicked and caused an accident. "Please, please, please," she murmured.

Rebecca ignored the whispered pleading. Instead, she concentrated on the chess game playing out on the road ahead.

Within minutes she arrived at the barricade, farther back from where she had hoped. "We're here, David. The truck has flipped onto its side, blocking the road."

David stood, leaning forward for a quick look. "We can figure something out. Is the other crew here?"

"Dispatch, we are at the transfer point," Rebecca said, then identified their unit number.

"Roger that. Start the transfer. The officer on-site will escort you."

"Mrs. Lapointe, please make sure you have all your belongings. We have a bit of a walk, and you won't be able to come back for them."

"I'm ready," she replied shakily.

Rebecca removed the keys and stepped out. She strode briskly to the rear and opened the back door. "All set then?" she asked her partner.

"Yep, let's do it."

As the stretcher was automatically lowered, the legs unfolded. David grabbed the back bar, and Rebecca gripped the front. "Let's go." Dangling from a metal pole affixed to the stretcher, the plastic IV bag swung back and forth in time with their rapid strides.

Cst. Swan pulled the barricade aside, "the roadway is blocked, but if you are careful, you can squeeze around the front of the cab. Watch your footing, the shoulder is soft, and the pavement is slippery with fuel and crushed grapes." As soon as the attendants, the stretcher carrying their patient, and the distressed woman, whom he assumed was the patient's wife, had passed, he replaced the barrier. "Can I help you somehow?" Swan asked.

David chinned toward the woman. "Make sure Mrs. Lapointe gets through okay."

"Will do," Swan said and moved toward her. "Mrs. Lapointe, if you put your coat on and give me the other things, that will free up your hands," he suggested.

"Yes, of course," she quickly handed him Nate's jacket and braced her purse between her knees while she slipped on her jacket. "I'm fine now," she pulled her purse strap over her shoulder.

"Okay, we have to be very careful where we walk."

"Cst. Swan, the ambulance crew has arrived from Penticton," a voice squawked through his shoulder mic.

"Roger that. We're on the way. Stay on your side of the obstruction. We'll be there in a few minutes," Swan replied while looking at David to confirm that he'd overheard the exchange.

"Good call."

Chapter 10

Penticton Regional Hospital

Tethered to the hospital bed by electronic cables and a monitor, Alan Fraser watched the two figures stride toward him. Cops. The guy walked like a cop, and yet, he was well-dressed and physically attractive, almost pretty. A chick magnet with short dark hair, deep dimples, and blue eyes. It was a wonder someone hadn't broken the guy's nose just to mess up that cute face.

The taller, red-haired woman seemed to be in charge. She was lean and attractive, with a commanding presence. *I bet she'd enjoy intimidating the crap outta guys with her gun and handcuffs.*

Thinking about the handcuffs and Emma, his occasional hookup, Fraser unconsciously sucked on his bottom lip. Once the doctor discharged him from the hospital, he'd call Emma for a ride to the warehouse where he'd parked his pickup. Maybe if he played his cards right, she'd come home with him and be his nurse with benefits until he recovered from his injuries.

"Mr. Fraser, I'm Cpl. Smith, General Investigative Section of the Penticton RCMP," the woman announced, then pointing at Ethan, she continued, "and this is Cst. Jones."

Fraser smirked at her. *Yep, a bossy pain in the ass. Introducing herself with a big fancy title, and then she wouldn't even let pretty-boy introduce himself.*

He shifted his features to display distress and suffering, "I'm in pain," Fraser groaned, holding one hand on his abdomen. "I'm really stressed. I was in danger of being burned alive in my truck," he whined. If he did this right, he could get more medication. His gut hurt, and he had bruises where the seatbelt had jerked him back against the seat and a bump on his forehead. He was stiff and sore from hanging upside-down in the cab until an ambulance attendant and a cop finally freed him.

"When was that? I didn't see or smell a fire," Caitlin said.

"My fuel tank was leaking, and the engine was still warm. It could have caught fire."

"But it didn't," she stated.

"No, but I'm a victim, too," he moaned. "It wasn't my fault. It was a bad situation involving the cyclists and a group of deer." There had been many different uniforms arrive, police, ambulance, and city workers, while he was trapped, but he hadn't seen much of what was going on with the people he'd hit.

"We just have a few questions to ask. We won't take long," she said, carefully keeping her expression neutral.

"Can you get the nurse? I need more drugs."

"I'll ask her to check on you when we leave," Caitlin noted that Fraser wasn't sweating, his breathing was regular, and his monitor showed normal blood pressure and pulse readings. He could wait a bit.

"Don't be so heartless," he moaned, fighting the urge to call the female cop a heartless bitch. "I need more drugs."

Caitlin pointedly looked at his monitor. "Your blood pressure and pulse rate seem normal to me, Mr. Fraser. None of the readings have activated the alarms to alert the medical staff, so I'm sure you'll be okay to answer my questions."

Perplexed, Fraser glanced at the monitor. "How do you know that?"

"My father is a doctor," she said.

"You don't know. I could have internal bleeding."

"Internal bleeding would be obvious with an increase in your pulse rate and drop in your blood pressure. Just answer a few quick questions, and we'll leave."

"How are the other people?" he asked, belatedly expressing concern. "Are they badly injured?"

"We'll get to that in a minute," Caitlin responded. If he was unaware that he had killed the two women, she could use that to her advantage.

"Do I need my lawyer?"

"That's up to you, sir, but it would be simpler if you answered our questions."

"Fine. Ask your damn questions, then get me the nurse."

"Cst. Jones will record our discussion on his cell phone and take notes for accuracy. Mr. Fraser, what were you doing when your truck struck the cyclists?"

"Driving." *What the hell did she think I was doing?*

Caitlin imagined giving him a sharp slap on his head, like her father's old-school response to her biting, teenage sarcasm. Instead, she clamped down on her annoyance and asked, "driving from where to where?"

"Black Sage Road in Oliver with a load of grapes headed to Dream Chaser Winery, not far from where those people just cycled right out in front of my vehicle."

"You say they cycled in front of you?"

"Yeah, they didn't even look, just moved into my lane. I didn't have time to brake. I was terrified." Pretending that he was feeling emotional, he wiped his dry eyes with the corner of the sheet.

"And then what happened?"

"I stomped the brake pedal, and the trailer jackknifed," he said. "The next thing I know, the unit flopped over and slid across the road." He clamped a hand over his abdomen and moaned, "I need to get more meds. I'm suffering here."

Both Caitlin and Jones flicked their eyes to the monitor. No change in his vitals. Everything looked completely normal. "Just a few more minutes," she said, ignoring his plea. "When a trailer jackknifes, isn't that an indication of sudden and forceful braking while traveling at high speed?" Caitlin knew the answer was yes, and was interested in how he'd try to justify speeding.

"Well, I might have been a little over the speed limit. It's 60, but the traffic always moves along at about 70. I don't want to cause a backup of impatient drivers who might try to pass me. Naramata Road is narrow and winding, passing can be dangerous, so I go with the flow."

"So, you were speeding to prevent other drivers from causing an accident? Is that what you are saying?" She pretended to believe him.

"Yeah," Fraser nodded, pleased she had bought his excuse. "Yeah, that's right. I was being a good citizen."

He's dumber than a sack of hammers.

"Actually, Mr. Fraser, the speed limit is still 50 kilometers per hour until just before the corner, and then it drops to 30 kilometers coming into the corner where you ran into the cyclists," Caitlin said. "You were, by your admission traveling at the very least 40 kilometers per hour over the speed limit," she paused, "and we have two witnesses who say you were driving well over the speed limit when you passed them."

"What witnesses?" he demanded, then added, "wait, no, I didn't say that I was driving at 70 km. I said sometimes I do to keep the traffic flowing and not jamming up behind me," he sputtered, "you're trying to put words in my mouth." The last time he'd looked at his speedometer, he'd been traveling at 90 km, but no way in hell was he ever going to admit that. "I want a lawyer!" He shouted.

And with those words, Caitlin knew the interview was over. "Then please bring your lawyer with you when we take your formal statement at the detachment."

Surprised, Fraser jerked involuntarily. "What do you mean, formal statement?"

"Mr. Fraser, you were involved in a collision that claimed the lives of two people and seriously injured a third."

"No, that's not right." His face paled, and sweat appeared on his upper lip. "I didn't kill anyone. I could have died with them dodging in front of my truck like that."

"Two women died because of the collision between your vehicle and their bicycles. Our investigation will be lengthy and thorough," Caitlin stated. "Upon your release from the hospital, you are required to make a signed statement at the RCMP detachment."

"Sure," he shrugged. "Whenever I feel up to it."

"This is a homicide investigation, Mr. Fraser. There is a police member standing guard until the doctor discharges you." She moved the curtain and pointed at the watchful woman standing in the hallway of the emergency ward. "Then the officer will take you directly to our station for your interview."

"You can go to hell! I'm a sick man." He grabbed his gut again for effect.

"Depending on the results of the blood tests you may be facing serious charges," she said. "Don't even think about leaving the hospital without your police escort. That will only compound your difficulties." Caitlin nodded at Jones, indicating she was done.

"We'll see you soon, Mr. Fraser," Jones said as he sketched a wave.

Fraser gave Jones a dark look.

Stepping into the corridor, Caitlin smiled at the constable. "Hey Nat, do you need anything before we head back to the station?"

"Nope, I'm all good. Any idea how long I'll be guarding him?" Cst. Natalie Garcha asked.

"I'm not sure, a few hours anyway until the doctor does rounds again and either releases him or moves him upstairs into a proper ward."

"We'd still be watching him in the ward, right?"

"Yep, we want him under observation at all times, and then he gets escorted to the station for booking," Caitlin confirmed. "I'll ensure the watch commander sends a replacement every four hours." She pointed at a chair. "No need to stand. Get comfortable, but keep alert," she lowered her voice. "I don't trust this guy. He might try to leave."

"Okay, thanks," Natalie pulled the chair over and sat, looking directly at the curtained booth

Crushed

where Fraser lay, moaning loudly. "Is he badly injured?" she whispered to Caitlin.

"He thinks he's dying," Jones grinned.

Caitlin shot a warning look at Jones, telling him to keep his voice down, "his vital signs all looked normal to me. In any case, he has a call button close at hand, so don't leave your post to go and find a nurse or doctor. He's quite capable of summoning assistance, but I suspect he's overplayed his discomfort, and the nurses have been told to ignore his demands for more medication."

"Got it," Natalie said.

"Is your dad really a doctor?" Jones quietly asked Caitlin.

One side of her mouth tipped up in a sardonic grin. "Psychiatrist."

"Cheeky," he laughed.

"Catch you later, Nat," Caitlin lifted her hand in a brief wave, then walked toward the exit.

Crossing the parking lot to their cruiser, Caitlin heard the wail of a siren as it increased in volume. She paused and watched the tableau of the vehicle rocking to a stop, the attendants hurrying to unload the patient, and two medical staff rushing out to assist. She could hear the staccato rush of words as the attendant updated the doctor. "Possible stroke, leading to cardiac arrest."

A frantic woman shouted, "Nathan! Nathan! Honey, don't leave me." The jacket clutched in her hand dropped to the ground.

Watching the scenario unfold, Caitlin said to Jones. "Dispatch will call us if the situation needs to be investigated."

Crushed

Chapter 11

Penticton Morgue

Gently rubbing the hand of the deceased woman, Dr. Elizabeth Kennedy spoke softly. "I'm sorry to make your acquaintance under these circumstances, Lorna. This isn't the best place to make new friends. I'll take good care of you and your daughter, Camden."

Cst. Ethan Jones shivered. When he dressed for work this morning, he'd forgotten it was his turn to do morgue duty, and his stylish leather jacket was not up to the job. He'd left his heavier jacket hanging on the back of his chair at the station. The ambient temperature inside the morgue wasn't much warmer than the November morning lurking outside the door. The chilly environment only slightly diminished the odors, the smell of death, and chemicals.

In the background, a mellow country artist sang about smooth Tennessee whiskey and sweet strawberry wine. Chris Stapleton? Yes, that was his name. It was an interesting choice of music to listen to while performing a post-mortem. However, in his opinion, music of any genre would never mask the heartbreak of what the pathologist dealt with calmly and efficiently, day in and day out. Not unlike his job, he supposed, just a different environment. As a police officer, he was exposed to all types of violence. Murder. Domestic abuse. Child abuse. Gang activities and more, yet he was sure he wouldn't have the courage to dissect bodies to investigate the cause of death. A quiver of revulsion slithered up his spine, and he shivered again.

Dr. Kennedy noticed his reaction and ignored it. Cst. Jones had attended her autopsies before and hadn't fainted or dashed white-faced from the room. He'd hold it together and be professional.

Jones quietly watched as she continued to chat with Lorna Sinclair as if she could still hear and understand. Curious, he asked, "why do you talk to the corpses, Dr. Kennedy?"

"It's my way of showing respect." Under the unrelenting lights, her pale blue eyes looked gray, like her eyebrows and the few pieces of short gray hair that poked out from under her paper cap. The corners of her eyes crinkled as she smiled at Jones from behind her surgical mask. "I grew up in a church-going family, so even though the scientist in me rejects the concept of heaven and hell, a small part of me would like to assist her onward to her next destination."

"That's an interesting belief," Jones said.

She gently lifted a blood-soaked piece of blonde hair from Sinclair's face. "She is an attractive woman," she said. "Now, let's get started. Lorna Sinclair is forty-one years of age.

She appears to be in good physical health, with good muscle tone and little body fat."

"She and her two teenagers are, were, avid cyclists," Jones interjected.

Kennedy nodded; she'd heard his comment. She ran her hands over Sinclair's skull, "she has a skull fracture, and," she slid her hands lower to the vertebrae in Sinclair's neck, "and a C1–C2 fracture, which is the likely cause of death." She indicated the two cervical vertebrae closest to the skull. "A fracture in this location is most often fatal, or so life-changing that if the patient survived, they'd often wish it had been fatal."

"As in, the person would be paralyzed?"

"Yes, most likely a quadriplegic." Kennedy's hands probed further, feeling for anomalies in Sinclair's arms, ribcage, and legs. "She has several fractures and injuries consistent with being struck at speed by a large vehicle."

Jones scribbled a few notes as the pathologist spoke. He struggled to keep his mind focused on the mundane task. Meaghan and he had cycled that same route dozens of times, feeling the whoosh of air nudge their bodies when a vehicle sped past on the narrow winding road. From now on, they would stick to the relative safety of the graveled Trans Canada Trail. The popular bike path traversed the vineyards and orchards on the old Kettle Valley Railway, crossed the roadway near Hillside Estate Winery, and climbed steadily to the tunnels before eventually winding into the city of Kelowna. He wasn't about to orphan their infant son, Rowan, because of a bike ride. Behind his paper mask, his mouth tweaked as he visualized Rowan's gurgling laugh and drooling smile. Jones had only been lukewarm about having a family until Rowan arrived. He was a heart-melting addition to their family unit, and now, he couldn't imagine a life without his son.

"Ethan?"

"I'm sorry, Dr. Kennedy," Jones stammered. "I was thinking about our son Rowan and how awful it would be to lose him or for us to die before he had grown into manhood."

"I understand completely," she said. "I just asked if you wanted a full tox screen on Mrs. Sinclair."

His eyebrows cinched together. "Do you think it's necessary?"

"Probably not," she said, "but this is wine country, and cyclists have been known to be inebriated from wine tasting at various wineries along the Naramata Bench."

"Good point. Then please check for drugs and alcohol."

"Are you staying for the next bit when I open her up?" She reached for a Stryker saw.

His eyes darted downward, then tentatively met Kennedy's. "Must I?"

She studied him for a moment, "no, I am quite confident that my original assessment of a C1-C2 fracture is the cause of death. I'll text you if I find anything that contradicts my findings."

"Do you know when the autopsy for Camden Sinclair will be?"

"She will be later this afternoon. I'll text you with a time."

Jones made a mental note to let Caitlin take that one. Watching the teenager being dissected would be too much for him. "Thank you so much, Dr. Kennedy."

"Liz."

"Thank you, Liz." He smiled.

"And someday, I want to meet your son, Rowan."

"Yes, but not here," Jones anxiously blurted, thinking he wouldn't survive seeing his son lying on her autopsy table.

Elizabeth Kennedy watched a range of emotions flicker across Ethan's attractive features. Pride because she had expressed interest in his baby Rowan. Sadness and fear that someday Rowan might be in this very room. She smiled reassuringly at Jones. "No, Ethan, I don't ever want to meet Rowan here in my office."

Chapter 12

Front Street Penticton

Standing in the cozy Honey Toast Bakery Café on Front Street, Jessica inhaled the scents of cinnamon and warm chocolate that wafted toward her from the glass-fronted case containing trays of freshly baked scones, muffins, pies, and banana bread. Heaven. Second, only to enjoying fresh croissants and café au lait on an ancient, sun-warmed terrace in southern France. And third, on her list of blissful mornings was a freshly brewed cup of coffee on the beach in Mexico while watching the giant sea turtles lay their eggs at sunrise.

The café had tables and chairs inside for perhaps twelve patrons and about the same on the streetside deck. The inside seats were taken, and the patio in November was too cool for her, but that didn't matter as she had plans to share her purchase with Mike in their comfy cottage. Scones and a freshly made latte with a drizzle of caramel sauce would be a soothing treat for her battered soul.

Sleep had eluded her for most of the night. Troubling images of Lorna's still body had revolved mercilessly in her brain, the blood pooling around Camden, the battered truck lying on its side, and the scattered bins of grapes. And the smells, God, the smells of their broken bodies and the diesel fuel.

She'd spent most of the night wrapped in a blanket on the sofa, with Sparky's chin on her lap. Twice during the night, Mike had sleepily padded from their bed to the couch, wrapping her in his arms and murmuring in her ear. It took some convincing, but eventually he went back to bed.

Straight from her sleepless night, she had arrived at the police station to give her statement to Caitlin, followed by an hour of carting their belongings from the hotel to the car. Mike had a busy morning scheduled at the winery and couldn't leave to help her move out of the Ramada. She was exhausted. Frayed and irritable.

"Hi Jess, what can I get you today?" The attractive brunette playfully clacked the metal bakery tongs imitating a lobster claw, or maybe a giant crab.

"Oh, hi, Kate. I was daydreaming about warm and sunny locations." She mechanically smiled at the young woman standing behind the counter. "Four scones, please," Jessica said.

"What flavors would you like today?" Kate asked. "And what exotic places were you daydreaming about?"

"Surprise me, mix it up." She didn't have the energy to choose. "I was thinking about southern France and Mexico."

"Both of those places are on my bucket list," Kate responded, rapidly picking out four plump scones and lifting them into a bakery box with her tongs, "and here you go," she tucked the end flaps, closed the lid, and placed the box on the counter in front of Jessica. "The scones are fresh out of the oven and still warm."

"They smell divine. I'll pay with my Visa."

"Isn't it terrible about Lorna and Camden Sinclair?" Kate said as she rang up Jessica's purchase.

Surprised, Jessica blinked rapidly, willing away the threat of tears. It was a small community. She should have known people would gossip about the double tragedy. She aimed her card at the reader. "Yes, it's terrible."

Kate dropped her voice. "You were friends, weren't you?"

"We're business acquaintances," she replied, downplaying her relationship. She didn't want to be drawn into a long gossipy chat about the carnage she'd witnessed. Opening her wallet, she concentrated on slotting her credit card back into its usual place. Her hands trembled as she tucked the wallet into her pocket.

"And Tyler was injured. I think he's still in the hospital."

"How awful," Jessica replied, refusing to add any information. She wanted to grab her purchase and escape.

"Yes. And I heard there was another emergency call during the road closure. A man had a heart attack, or a stroke, or something like that, and had to be rushed to the hospital, and I'm not sure if he made it in time." Suddenly realizing that the background chatter of café patrons had quieted and the customers were intently listening to her story, Kate's face pinked with embarrassment. She hurried to hand Jessica her receipt and her purchase. "If you see James or Tyler, please extend my condolences."

"Yes, of course, thank you." Jessica hustled outside and got into the car. Carefully placing the bakery box on the passenger seat, she braced her hands on the steering wheel, whispering, "Damn, damn, damn."

Sparky stood on the console between the front seats, nudging her cheek with his nose. "Don't worry, Sparky, I'm not upset at you. You're a very good boy," she said, giving him a quick hug. Concentrating on her breathing, she waited until the threat of tears had passed and called Mike.

He answered on the third ring, "hey beautiful, how are you doing?"

"Hi, my love. I just finished moving our things out of the hotel. I'll be home in about twenty minutes," she said.

"Good." Hearing the tremor in her voice, he asked, "is everything okay?"

"Not great. The gossip about yesterday's accident is spreading. I just got blindsided by a nice young woman that I know. She wanted to chat about the accident."

"I'm so sorry, Jess, but gossiping is human nature."

"As I discovered," she said, absently running a finger along the car's dashboard, sweeping up the accumulation of dog hair and dust. "Right, well, I won't be long," she said, "and I bought scones, from Honey Toast, as a treat."

"I'll organize coffee to go with the goodies," Mike said. "Drive safely, but don't dawdle! I love those scones."

"And again, we have to pass by the accident scene," Jessica murmured to Sparky as she eased her foot off the gas pedal. It was heartbreaking to hear that someone else had died, perhaps because of the delay.

Large temporary highway signs cautioning drivers to slow down to 20 kilometers per hour, the deep gouges in the pavement, and a dark stain on the road were silent reminders of two lives lost. Several large grape bins were stacked to the side, waiting for the owner to claim them. The mounds of squashed grapes had been washed aside, presumably by the fire department when they hosed the fuel off the roadway. By spring, the only noticeable reminder would be the significant gash in the large maple tree, yet she doubted she could ever drive past this spot without visualizing the disaster.

Until yesterday, whenever the need arose, she had buzzed back and forth between Naramata and Penticton without realizing there wasn't another route between the two communities. Many narrow side roads dead-ended at properties that overlooked the lake and didn't connect laterally.

Yesterday was chaotic for residents and tourists because of the lengthy closure while the tragedy was thoroughly documented, investigated, and the damaged vehicle removed. Never mind the inconvenience, it was heartbreaking to learn that someone else may have died on the way to the hospital, perhaps because of the delay.

She needed a sugary treat to revitalize her energy and take her mind away from yesterday's horror, if only for a few minutes.

Chapter 13

Penticton RCMP Station

"That's interesting," Caitlin said as she read the emailed copy of the autopsy report. She leaned back in her chair and rested the heels of her boots on the desk, partly for comfort and partly because her habit annoyed Ethan Jones, her fastidious partner.

Jones looked up, saw her boots, set his jaw, and pointedly ignored her obnoxious habit. "What's interesting?" he asked.

"Zero indication of alcohol in Lorna Sinclair's blood. And no drugs or even over-the-counter medications. Nothing."

He shrugged. "So?"

"Other than the obvious, she wasn't impaired. It's unusual. Most people self-medicate with Ibuprofen, Aspirin, or Advil. Something."

"Maybe she was concerned about staying healthy."

"Still," Caitlin made a face, "it's odd."

"Is it important to our case?"

"It's a piece of the puzzle that we are trying to solve." Caitlin picked up the second report. "The daughter, Camden Sinclair, died from massive internal injuries and a ruptured aorta. No signs of any drugs or alcohol, but she had some Ibuprofen in her system."

"So, not likely that either woman lost control of their bicycle or fell into the path of the truck?"

"I don't think that's what happened, despite Fraser telling us the cyclists veered in front of his truck," Caitlin said. "We have the witness statements from Charles and Mary Simpson. Fraser was tailgating their car, and then he sped past when Charles pulled onto the shoulder."

"And according to this, Alan Fraser was impaired," Ethan said, brandishing another report.

"Alcohol? Swan said he didn't notice alcohol on Fraser's breath when he checked him at the scene, but that's not a foolproof test."

"A minor amount of alcohol, but a lot of meth and cocaine."

"So, we can charge him with impaired driving, for now."

"Not much comfort for the Sinclair family, though," Ethan responded.

Caitlin stood and stretched, working out the kinks in her back and shoulders, then reached down, and scrolled through the headlines of the online news services. "Remember the ambulance arriving at the hospital after we interviewed Fraser?"

"Yeah."

"Their patient Nathan Lapointe succumbed to a stroke."

"That's too bad."

"I mentioned it because he lived in Naramata, and the road was closed due to the accident caused by Fraser."

"Allegedly caused by Fraser."

"Sure. Allegedly. The Naramata ambulance crew had to walk the stretcher past the accident site and transfer Mr. Lapointe to a second ambulance, thereby losing valuable time before arriving at the hospital."

Jones let his hands drop to the desk, thinking about this new information, "does that make Fraser responsible for his death too?"

"It's definitely something to ask Sarge," Caitlin agreed. "Are you coming?"

"Where?"

"To see if Sarge has five minutes, and then I'm going to the Sinclairs' home. I checked with the hospital and Tyler has been released. I want to chat with him first, then privately tell James of the autopsy results."

"You go ahead. I'm tracking Alan Fraser's movements leading up to the accident."

"I'll be back in about an hour," she strode to Sergeant Williams' office and rapped on the doorframe of his already open door.

"Enter," he barked. Unless he was involved in a sensitive meeting, Williams typically left his door open and kept one ear tuned to the background chatter in the station. It was a talent that he'd fine-tuned over the years. He could listen to radio communications, one-sided phone conversations, and office gossip, and process his portion of the endless administrative paperwork.

"Good morning, boss."

When she first transferred to Penticton, Caitlin had been wary of Sarge's surly manner. He seemed perpetually angry, as if he had a terrible case of hemorrhoids, and sitting was excruciatingly painful. She had since discovered that his gruff exterior was a coping mechanism developed after years of being taunted by childhood bullies about his name: William Williams. *What were his parents thinking?* Recently Williams had admitted that if someone joked about his double name, he leaned closer and grinned like a Viking about to slit the throat of a rival warrior. She'd laughed at that image. It was marginally better than his previous confession that he liked to rest his hand on his gun holster and give the offender a crazy-Jack-Nicholson smile.

Sarge was in his early fifties and nearing his thirtieth anniversary as a cop, making him eligible for retirement soon. She knew Williams didn't golf, or fish, or hunt, and she wasn't convinced that playing with their grandbabies would be enough to keep his sharp mind occupied. The late-night stakeouts and junk food consumed in the police cruiser had thickened his waistline and rounded his shoulders. Deep crevices bracketed his wide mouth, set in a plain, almost homely face. His watchful dark eyes softened whenever he spoke of his wife Kyla and their happy brood of kids and grandbabies. Williams good-naturedly escorted Kyla to her many charity events, describing himself as her arm candy, her George Clooney. The first time Caitlin had heard his ironic assessment of his ordinary face and dad-body, she'd choked on her laughter.

"Yes?" Williams asked.

"Did you happen to read the online news this morning?"

"Yes, why?"

"Did you read the article about Nathan Lapointe dying from a stroke?"

"I skimmed it."

"When Jones and I were leaving PRH after interviewing Alan Fraser, our suspect in the death of Lorna and Camden Sinclair, we saw the ambulance arriving at the hospital."

Williams crossed his hands over his paunch and silently waited for her to continue.

"Nathan Lapointe lived in Naramata, and the ambulance crews were delayed because of the accident. He died. Can Alan Fraser be held accountable for his death too?"

"No," he shook his head, "not criminally at fault. The family can, however, initiate a civil lawsuit."

"Like the O.J. Simpson and Nicole Brown Simpson case?"

"Yes, like that one."

"O.J. was found guilty in the civil suit, but he argued against the decision, and the families haven't received much compensation."

Williams nodded, "sometimes it works out, and sometimes it doesn't. It's the only form of recourse open to the Lapointe family."

"Did you ever consider being a lawyer?" Caitlin asked. She knew he had a formidable intellect.

"Briefly. I hated school and couldn't imagine enduring three or four years in university, then working for another year as an articling student for eighty hours a week at a crappy wage rate."

Caitlin leaned closer to his desk. "Do they make less than a new cop?" she asked with a smile.

"Good point," Williams agreed with a rough laugh, "it's close. What's the status of this case?"

"We're checking Fraser's background and cross-referencing with Lorna and Camden Sinclair's information to see if they knew each other. There aren't any obvious connections between them. Neither Lorna nor her daughter Camden were impaired by alcohol or drugs. Fraser was."

Chapter 14

Summerland

Caitlin searched Google maps for the easiest route to the Sinclair home on Morrison Drive. The unfamiliar road wound past vineyards, wineries, and a whimsical animated outdoor display handcrafted with care by the homeowner.

Set back from the road, the Sinclair home was surrounded by more vineyards with a pleasant, east-facing, and unobstructed view of Okanagan Lake. Painted in neutral colors, the house looked well-maintained. A basketball hoop was mounted above the garage door. The front door was painted a deep shiny red outlined by white trim. Two flower beds flanked the entrance walkway showcasing a colorful late autumn display of hardy chrysanthemums, daisies, and marigolds. And kale? Caitlin pulled a face. In her opinion, it was the only suitable application for that vile-tasting vegetable; planted in an entrance garden.

From the outside, the house looked like a happy place for a happy family, not a home containing heartbreak and sorrow. She parked her police vehicle behind Sinclair's dark blue truck and swung her legs onto the driveway.

She rang the doorbell and stood where she was visible through the door cam. "Good afternoon, Mr. Sinclair," she said when he answered the door. "I'm Cpl. Caitlin Smith, General Investigative Section of the Penticton RCMP. May I come in, sir?"

He nodded listlessly and stepped back, allowing her to enter.

"I am sorry for your loss, Mr. Sinclair," she said. "How are you holding up?"

"Surviving." James Sinclair wore clean clothes, his hair was combed, and he'd recently shaved, but the dark circles under his eyes and a sallow complexion pointed to a lack of sleep. The sweet odor of stale alcohol hung over him, so thick she imagined a fog draped over his shoulders.

As he firmly closed and locked the door, he noticed her questioning glance. "It's a new routine," he stated. "One of my overly helpful neighbors has developed an infuriating habit. She rings the doorbell, and if I don't answer it quickly enough to satisfy her, she barges inside, shouting my name as if I'm an invalid who needs home care." He spat the words. "She's upsetting my son, and he needs his rest."

"Yes, I can see how that would be disconcerting," she empathized. "Would you like me to remove my boots?" She pointed at her sturdy footwear.

"Don't bother," he said, "the kitchen is down the hall." He gestured listlessly toward the other side of the house.

Wiping her boots on the mat, she followed Sinclair deeper inside the home. "And your son, Tyler? How is he doing?" The kitchen stank of rotting food and a garbage bin that needed to be emptied. Splotches of spilled liquids dotted the countertops and the floor. A greasy frying pan lay in the sink. An empty pizza box lay on the table—no wonder he didn't want his neighbors inviting themselves into his house.

Sinclair scooped up the empty pizza box and self-consciously stuffed it in the cupboard under the sink. "He's coping," he said as he pulled out a chair, "have a seat."

"Thank you," Caitlin sat and scootched the chair closer to the table. "I was hoping to speak to Tyler briefly to clarify some of his information."

"He's asleep, and I don't want to wake him. Our doctor has prescribed a mild sedative so that he could rest."

"I understand. This is such a difficult time for both of you."

"Yes, it is."

Laying her hand on her bag, she held Sinclair's gaze, "I have the preliminary autopsy report for both your wife and daughter. If you prefer, I could summarize it for you."

He nodded curtly.

"I'll speak softly so that I don't disturb Tyler," she said, meaning she didn't want his son to overhear the gruesome details.

Sinclair waved a hand dismissively. "He won't hear you. He'll be asleep for at least six more hours."

There was no easy way to do this. Caitlin pulled the autopsy report out of her bag and self-consciously licked her bottom lip. She spoke clearly and quietly, "Mrs. Sinclair died of a fracture in this area." Her fingers moved to the base of her skull, where it joined the spine. "Death would have been instantaneous."

His sallow complexion paled to white. He clamped a hand over his mouth and bent forward, his elbows resting on his knees.

Caitlin waited, hesitating between the urge to comfort the man and remaining professionally detached.

"Please continue," he mumbled from behind his hand.

"Her tox screen was clear. She wasn't inebriated."

Sinclair's head snapped up. "Of course she wasn't! She's been in AA for ten years. She won't take a damn thing, even when she's in pain," he objected hotly, then looked away. "I mean, she wouldn't take anything when she was in pain," he softly amended.

"Thank you for that piece of information. We didn't know that she was in AA."

James breathed deeply, then tentatively met her eye. "And my daughter, Camden?"

She had been dreading this moment. "She died from internal injuries and a loss of blood."

"So, not quick."

"I'm very sorry, sir."

His shoulders shuddered violently as he sobbed into his hands, "you make sure you get that bastard, and soon!"

"We're diligently pursuing the evidence, sir."

"He'd better not get off on a technicality, or I'll deal with him."

"Mr. Sinclair." Annoyed, Caitlin straightened her posture and stared at the top of Sinclair's head. "Issuing threats does not help. In fact, it could land you in trouble. Just let us do our job."

He snatched a tissue from the box and loudly blew his nose. "You just make sure you get him."

Changing tactics, she asked, "is there someone I can call for you, Mr. Sinclair?"

"No, just leave."

Caitlin stood. "Are you sure I can't call someone to be with you, sir?"

His shoulders drooped, and his eyes were pointed at the floor. "Please. Just go," he whispered.

"Again, I'm so sorry for your loss." As she walked toward the front door, Caitlin quickly poked her head into the living room. A pillow and blankets were stacked on the sofa. Bottles, cans, and empty glasses littered the coffee table. The house reeked of despair, sadness, and grief. A family shattered.

Chapter 15

Summerland

James Sinclair sloppily splashed more whiskey into his glass. He'd lost track. Was this his third, fourth, or maybe his fifth tonight?

The autopsy results had been a shock. It had been so clinical, so final. The pathologist's report stated that Lorna had died quickly while Camden had died slowly from blood loss. His poor baby girl—helpless and dying. Listening as her world faded away. And he hadn't even known that they were dead until their bodies were at the morgue waiting for official identification. He should have been there to hold them, tell them they were loved, and tell them that life without them was meaningless.

His index finger flicked at the screen on his phone. "So sorry for your loss. Our condolences. Big healing hugs. They are missed. We're here for you. Keeping you in my prayers." And on and on, kind, well-meaning, but at the same time, empty messages from hundreds of acquaintances. Words would never repair his or Tyler's shattered hearts.

He choked back a sob and tipped the glass, sucking in a gulp of whiskey. He should stay sober for Tyler, but he couldn't breathe without the pain-numbing effects of alcohol. He wouldn't get out of bed if it weren't for his son. Instead, he would very deliberately drink himself to death.

Heaving a sigh, he reached for one of the many photo albums that Lorna had created. In a world of digital photos that rarely escaped the electronic confines of phones, she had persisted with printing her favorites and preserving them in photo albums, along with concert ticket stubs, maps, and brochures. It was her way of preserving the history of their busy lives.

His hot tears splattered on the plastic-covered pages as he relived the family holidays and road trips. Camden's first day in Grade 1, and middle school, then moving on to high school. Camden would never graduate. Marry. Have her own family. Be an auntie.

Screaming, he heaved the photo album across the room, smashing a Murano glass vase into a shower of thin glittering shards. It was their one souvenir of an expensive tenth-anniversary trip to Italy. He stumbled over to the mess and sunk to his knees. "Lorna, my love, I am so, so sorry," he slurred as he picked up the bigger bits, oblivious to the glass slicing his fingers and knees.

"Dad!" Tyler's groggy voice called out from his bedroom on the upper floor of their home, "Dad, what's happening? Do you need my help?"

"I'm fine, son." Surprised that Tyler had awoken from the sedative, James concentrated on speaking clearly. "You shouldn't be up. Go back to bed," he said to Tyler. His son had a cast from foot to hip, stabilizing his fractured femur, and navigating the stairway was difficult. He didn't want Tyler tumbling down the stairs to comfort him, the supposed adult.

James swayed as he reached for the album. The spine of the three-ring binder had broken, spilling the pages in a disorderly pile on the floor. "Sweetheart, I'm so sorry. You would be so disappointed with me," he mumbled as he bent over and pushed the stiff pages into an untidy heap. A bit of paper peaked out from behind a large photo. He peeled back the plastic overlay and gently pulled on the corner of the hidden paper. It was a photo, one he hadn't seen before. Lorna and another man, arms wound tightly around each other and smiling into each other's eyes, like lovers.

He dropped onto the couch and stared at the photo. "Who's this?" He flipped it over and read the pencil notation. *Mitchell, 2007.* "What the hell?"

"Dad? Are you sure everything is okay?" Tyler's voice was closer. He was now at the top of the stairway.

Worried Tyler might see the photo, James stuffed it under a cushion and hurried to the bottom of the stairs "Hey, sport, what're you doing out of bed? I thought the drugs the doctor gave you would help you sleep."

"I was asleep when I heard the loud noise. I wanted to make sure you were okay. Are you okay, Dad?" Tyler was still working out how to manage the crutches, and feeling wobbly, he steadied himself by leaning against the railing.

"I'm fine." James tried to reassure his son with a smile, but his lips wouldn't cooperate. "It's just hard," he whispered.

Tyler nodded and swiped at the tears on his face. "Yeah, I know, Dad. I miss them too."

James climbed the stairs, two at a time, and wrapped the grieving teenager in his arms. "Me too, son, me too."

"Please take care of yourself, Dad. I couldn't bear to lose you too," Tyler quietly added, "you've been drinking a lot lately."

"Yes, I know, son and I promise to do better," he said, yet again, the words that no one in the family believed anymore. "I promise." How many times had he made that same empty promise to Lorna?

"Okay. Sure, Dad."

"Let's get you back to bed."

"No worries, I can do it by myself."

"Don't be a tough guy. Let me help."

"Okay, but don't try to read me a bedtime story." Tyler's attempt at humor gripped James' aching heart.

Downstairs, James found the broom and dustpan and tackled the mess in the living room. He turned on all the lamps and the overhead light to see the shards of glass. Sweeping up the largest pieces, he inspected the floor and noticed dozens of tiny fragments glinting in the light. He swore softly, then pulled the vacuum out of a storage cupboard and plugged it in. Pushing the sofa away from its usual spot, he noticed two more glass bits. "Grow up. You have a son who needs you. No more raging benders," he rebuked himself as he thoroughly cleaned the living room rug and floor.

Twenty minutes later, he turned off the lights, wearily moved his pillow to one end of the sofa, and spread the blankets, creating a place to sleep. Sleeping in their bedroom wasn't possible and might never be possible again.

The unfamiliar photo of his wife and a man named Mitchell lay forgotten under the sofa cushion.

Tyler lay stiffly awake on his bed, tears rolling down both cheeks as he listened to his dad stumble around downstairs. He had heard the crash of something substantial hitting the floor, and now his dad was attempting to clean up the mess.

The vacuum started, and he listened as his dad pushed it back and forth in the living room. The vase, that big glass one that his mom loved so much. She had bought it in Italy on one of the few trips his parents had taken without Camden and himself.

The vacuum shut off. Tyler listened as his dad rummaged around, organizing the blankets and pillows for another night of restless sleep. The downstairs toilet flushed, then the noises stilled, leaving only the sound of the furnace rumbling to life.

Tyler jammed a pillow over his face to muffle his sobbing. His body quaked with grief, sending shots of pain into his damaged leg, but the physical pain was easier to withstand than the shredding of his heart. He was tired and sore, but sleep was elusive even after taking the prescribed sedative. The sound of the truck smashing into his family repeatedly played in his head like a discordant tune that wouldn't stop. He wanted to puke, but the effort to get out of bed again was too much. He swallowed hard, pushing the vile liquid down.

"Mom," he sobbed. "How are we going to survive without you and Camden?"

Chapter 16

On the Edge Winery

"Good morning, Mrs. Crawford," Jessica chirped while hanging her jacket on a hook behind the door.

Danielle Crawford had a classic beauty inherited from her ancestors in Languedoc, France. Her dark hair, cut in a shoulder-length bob, was streaked with silver. She shook her head good-naturedly and smiled. "Good morning, Jessica. We are neighbors, so please call me Danielle. Mrs. Crawford is my much older mother-in-law, not me."

"I'm sorry, my mom drilled it into her three offspring to always be respectful," Jessica said. "I'll try to remember." Jessica smiled, then deliberately added, "Danielle."

"Good. Let me show you how we do things in the wine shop."

"Actually, I've watched your summer staff, and the only thing I'm unfamiliar with is the point-of-sale system."

"It's straightforward. Come, I'll show you."

Crushed

Within twenty minutes, Jessica was comfortable with her new duties, "I think I've got it now if you want to carry on with your office work."

"There's no rush. The invoices and bank statements aren't going anywhere. I would like to know, how are you doing?" Danielle asked, laying her slim hand on Jessica's forearm. "I know you found Lorna and Camden after the accident."

"I'm fine," she lied, swiping at her eyes. "Sorry, let me find a tissue or something."

Danielle removed her hand, "I'm sorry I've upset you, Jess. Look behind the counter. I usually keep some on hand."

"No, please don't apologize. I can usually keep my emotions under control," Jessica said, grabbing the box and yanking out a wad of tissues. One was never enough for her messy nose; she preferred using sturdier paper towels. "I'm having trouble sleeping at night, but during the day, I keep busy and push everything away." She honked noisily into the clump of paper and roughly wiped her nose. She chucked the wet balled-up mess into the small garbage can, tucked under the counter.

Sighing, Danielle nodded. "Yes, I understand completely."

"I can't imagine what you and Dr. Crawford have gone through this year."

Danielle held out her hand for the tissue box and gracefully removed only two tissues. She lightly blew her nose, dabbed at the tip, and placed the used tissues in the same garbage can.

"Mrs. Crawford, Danielle." Jessica hastily corrected herself. "May I ask, is Katherine still being held in prison?"

"Yes, she is being held on a charge of conspiracy to commit murder." Her face crumpled. "She sold her home to pay her legal bills and now has some money in the bank, so the court has decided that she is a flight risk and must remain incarcerated until her trial."

"But they took her passport, right?"

"Yes. The prosecutor is concerned that since Katherine knows people like Volkov, she would be able to purchase a fake passport and move to another country, one without an extradition treaty."

Jessica was about to ask how Dr. Crawford was doing when she heard the slam of one, or maybe two, car doors, "it sounds like we have customers. I've got this," she said.

"Right, I'll return to my office before anyone spots me," Danielle said. "If I start chatting with the customers before I know it, the day is over while my tedious government reports remain unfinished.

"I'm pretty good at completing mind-numbing reports if you ever want to shuffle some of them over to me."

A grateful smile lit Danielle's face. "You might regret your offer," she said as the winery's front door cracked open.

"Hi, anyone here?"

"Yes, please come in," Jessica called out. Danielle sidled out, heading upstairs to her office on the second floor.

At one in the afternoon, Danielle peaked around the corner. "I'm going to pop over to the house and make a bite of lunch for Keegan and myself," she said. "May I bring you a sandwich when I come back?" Only Jessica was in the shop, and she was busy restocking the display racks.

"I'm good, thanks so much. I had a big breakfast, and that'll do me until dinner time."

"Okay, I'll be about an hour." As Danielle exited the side door closest to her home, she heard another car arrive in the driveway. November wasn't typically a busy time for sales, but they usually sold enough that it was worthwhile to have at least one employee available. She heard Jessica greet the customers, and then the heavy door shut off the exchange.

"Hi there, how are you today?" Jessica asked the group of four, two men and two women.

"We are fine, thank you," a blonde woman answered stiffly.

"Would you like to try some of our wines?" Jessica held a bottle of white wine in her hands; a sampling typically started with white and progressed to red.

The woman turned to the heavy-set man on her right and whispered to him. She nodded before answering. "Yes."

Consciously keeping a friendly smile on her face, Jessica placed four glasses on the countertop and poured a small measure into each as she started a spiel about the wine, the flavors they might taste, how the wine was aged, and what type of foods this wine complemented. Oddly the group was unresponsive, not engaging in the usual back-and-forth banter of typical wine enthusiasts. She might be new to this job, but she wasn't unfamiliar with the wines and how to promote them.

Only the blonde woman answered for the group when Jessica held up another bottle and said, "next is our award-winning Pinot Gris." Maybe, she reasoned, the woman is the only one who understands English, although she wasn't translating everything Jessica said, and the others weren't turning to the blonde with inquisitive looks or questions. They drank the samples and, without any change in their expressions, replaced the glasses on the counter, waiting for the next pour.

Twice she caught the heavy-set man studying her, his dark hooded eyes partially hidden by thick eyebrows.

"We want a tour," The blonde flatly stated when Jessica had completed the sampling.

"Normally, we would be happy to give you a tour of the winery and the vineyards. Unfortunately, this is a busy time in our production area, and our winemaker has his equipment spread over the floor space," she answered with a conciliatory smile. "I'm so sorry. It's not safe for visitors to enter the buildings." Mike had explicitly mentioned this situation at breakfast, stating he didn't want people touring through the winery for a few days.

A look of disdain settled on the features of the man who appeared to be the leader. "I will speak to Dr. Crawford," he stated.

"Dr. Crawford is recovering from an illness. Perhaps I could ask Mrs. Crawford to speak with you."

"Dr. Crawford."

"Sir, I am so sorry. I have been instructed not to disturb Dr. Crawford. May I ask Mrs. Crawford to meet with you?"

The man made a rude noise, turned on his heel, and stomped towards the door with his minions scurrying after him.

Jessica quickly phoned Mike, "hey, sweetie, a group of unhappy people might be headed your way. I told them no tours, but they weren't having it."

"I locked the doors this morning in case you forgot and tried to bring a group on a tour," he replied with a chuckle. "They won't get in." He spoke loudly over the background noise of the pumps. "Are you okay?"

"Yeah, I'm fine. I'll tell you all about it later."

Chapter 17

Olalla

Driving west on Highway 3A, a white Jeep sped past several small farms perched on the mountainside. The flatter land belonged to three prosperous-looking ranches comprised of a functional house, barns, and storage sheds, and stocked with fat black cattle. The rolling hills were claimed by a handful of newer architecturally designed homes on well-groomed acreages. In his experience, working ranches were messy but not chaotic. Hobby farms were tidy, with appearances being more important than the business of farming. On one side of the highway, the flatter land held grazing cattle, while the opposite side was strewn with large jagged boulders that had lost the fight with gravity and plunged from the peaks looming above.

The speed limit slowed from 90 to 70 kilometers an hour at the entrance to the tiny community of Olalla, and Ross anxiously scanned the collection of modest homes mixed with several mobile home parks. According to Google Maps, he was searching for a particular road that snaked off to the right and climbed into the craggy mountains blocking the late afternoon sun.

Zack's Town Trader seemed to be the only business still in operation, although it was hard to tell if it was still active. An eclectic assortment of rusting farm implements, a bicycle rickshaw, a red and white fountain built to resemble a hen-house, and a collection of old memorabilia lined a front porch. It covered most of the yard in front of the building. Off to one side, an old-fashioned massive wooden wine tank rested horizontally on the ground.

He turned onto what he hoped was the right road and exhaled with relief when he spotted a faded sign: Alan Fraser private property, NO trespassing. The narrow dirt track twisted deeper into the hills, passing broken fences, a handful of dispirited cows, and a slouching barn before ending at the home that hadn't felt the touch of a paintbrush in decades. The faded yellow paint was wholly worn away on the corners and window ledges. A discarded washing machine silently rusting on the porch kept company with a mysterious pile of metal junk.

He drove alongside the barn and backed into a concealed spot in the orchard, giving himself a quick departure route. Fraser was a known meth dealer who was unpredictable and volatile, and he probably had at least one gun inside the house.

Reaching across to the passenger seat, Ross grabbed a pair of old runners he had found in the back of his closet and stuffed his feet into the shoes. Slipping on a pair of nitrile gloves, he pulled a plastic bag out from under the seat, stepped out, and closed the driver's door. The farm was cast in deep shadows as the season advanced toward the winter solstice. He needed to get this done and be gone before dark. Lights at the house would be suspicious, although he had no idea if any other house overlooked this property.

Nervously scanning the area again, he advanced toward the house and banged on the front door. "Hey Alan, are you home? Alan, wake up, man! I've got something for you."

He sure as shit hoped the house was empty.

Earlier in the morning, he'd hung around the hospital, eavesdropping on the conversations between the staff. After being held in the hospital overnight for tests and observations, Alan Fraser was due to be released into the custody of the RCMP. He would be charged with DWI, driving while impaired, for now. Further charges depended on the results of his blood test.

The shocking death of Lorna Sinclair and her young daughter Camden had made the national news, and Ross had caught the quickest flight from Toronto to Vancouver. He planned to stash plenty of drugs in the house as a backup to the other charges Fraser was facing and then call in an anonymous tip. He wanted Fraser to be in jail for a very long time.

The front door was unlocked, still a common practice in many rural communities despite the rise in petty theft. Fraser had wrongly assumed that no one would bother him in this remote location.

Ross quickly scoped the house, checking for a hiding place that wouldn't be ridiculously easy to spot. A board squeaked as he walked through the larger bedroom. Kicking aside a grimy area rug, he noticed one board was loose and bent to pry it up.

"Well, well, it looks like I've found your stash. Let me give you an early Christmas bonus," he said, adding the bags of fentanyl, cocaine, and oxycodone that he'd purchased from several dealers in the Vancouver area. Replacing the board and the rug, he hurried out, shutting the door.

As he strode to the Jeep, a pair of headlights bounced through the valley, their beams breaking the deepening gloom. Another vehicle was coming up the gravel road. *Shit. Too soon.* He sighed and climbed back into his rental vehicle. There was no point in brazening it out by driving toward the incoming car. The dirt road was too narrow for two vehicles to pass. Fraser would know he had been at his house and could easily block his path to confront him.

As soon as Fraser got out of his vehicle, he would cut and run and hope the man didn't try to chase him down. Judging that he still had a few minutes before Fraser arrived, he got out of the Jeep, scooped up a handful of damp earth, and quickly smeared both license plates with mud. It wasn't much, but at least Fraser wouldn't be able to read the tags.

An older red truck drove within ten feet of the porch. Fraser turned off the ignition and slowly lowered his feet to the ground.

Fraser. Stiff and sore but mobile.

And alive.

That useless piece of dog shit was alive.

The white Jeep roared out of the orchard toward Fraser as he limped from his vehicle to the sagging porch of his shabby house. Ross would later wonder; how did that happen? How did he so easily discard his moral compass?

Startled by the menacing noise, Fraser half-turned, searching for the source, and tripped. He fruitlessly raised his arms to ward off the charging vehicle. "No!"

Ross felt a jarring thump as the front wheel smashed across Fraser's chest, followed by the rear wheel.

Howling with pain, Fraser slowly rolled onto his belly and strained to pull himself to the porch and the safety of his house.

Ross dispassionately watched the injured man in his side mirror, then moved the gearshift into reverse, took his foot off the brake, and stomped the gas pedal, accelerating across Fraser's back and shoulders. He put the Jeep in park and opened the door, listening. A faint pained groan came from under the vehicle.

Squatting down, he silently watched the dying man for a few minutes. "You're taking too long, buddy," he quietly said and got back in the vehicle. He drove over the body twice more before he was satisfied that Fraser was dead.

He turned the Jeep around and drove the single-track road towards the highway. His hands vibrated with fear. And horror. And adrenaline. He slammed on the brakes and bailed out of the cab, leaving the driver's door ajar. His ribs heaved as he puked in the bushes, over and over. Wiping the mess from his face, he sagged to the ground. "What the hell have I done?"

When that son-of-a-bitch Fraser tripped and fell, he couldn't control his rage. He had to kill him. Slowly pulling himself upright, he took a few deep breaths and shakily walked to the front of the vehicle, looking for damage. A quick glance confirmed that the plastic cowling under the grill was cracked and smeared with blood. There was probably more damage underneath, but nothing glaringly obvious.

He got back in the Jeep. Resting his hands on the steering wheel, he realized he was still wearing the nitrile gloves and the shoes that had left footprints in the house and yard. He changed his shoes and pulled off the gloves. *What was he going to do?*

Chapter 18

Highway 3A

Sitting at the stop sign, Ross glanced left, toward the route to Penticton where he could turn himself into the local RCMP. Then he looked right, to an escape route to Vancouver via highway 3A. He swung right. He desperately needed an unattended coin-operated car wash with high-pressure wands. He'd clean the Jeep the best he could, then drive the Hope-Princeton highway to Vancouver.

Ross noticed the roadway was damp from a brief rain shower that had passed through while he was inside Fraser's house. *Good.* The tires would create a fine mist of road grime, which might disguise the gore until he found a car wash. If he washed the vehicle a few times before he gassed it up and returned it to the rental company at the airport and then holed up in his hotel room until the departure time for his early morning flight to Toronto, he just might get away with it. It was a plan. A weak plan. But for the moment, his only plan.

Terrified of being pulled over, he set the cruise control to the speed limit and switched off the radio. He needed to be vigilant until he could get the Jeep washed at least once. He hadn't looked under the vehicle, but he was sure it was contaminated with blood and God knows what else. Hysteria bubbled up in his chest. What if something had snagged on the undercarriage, and he was dragging part of the body along the highway? Glancing repeatedly in the rearview mirror, it was too dark to see if there were marks on the road behind him.

Trembling, he thumbed the cruise control off and slowly steered to the side. Parking, he inhaled deeply and got out. He squatted and checked underneath. Nothing. He walked around the vehicle. It was too dark to see clearly.

Just keep driving, and find a car wash.

A short distance before Princeton, he powered down the passenger window, flung one shoe into the ditch, waited for a couple of miles, and tossed its mate.

That should take care of the footprint evidence in and around the house.

What about the drug dealers? Would any of them remember me?

With every buy, he had changed his hat, his shirt, and even his shoes. A cop friend had told him that few criminals considered their shoes as part of their disguise, and for some reason, that tidbit shared over pizza and beer had stuck in his mind. He'd also purposely made small buys from several dealers, male and female, from a mixture of the numerous gangs. With any luck, none of them would remember him, or if they did, they wouldn't cooperate with the police.

He couldn't think of anything he'd done, said, or worn, that screamed – remember me, I'm a murderer! When he'd decided to travel to B.C., he hadn't intended to kill Fraser, but seeing him alive had triggered a terrible overwhelming fury that had deadened his conscience. His vision truly had been clouded by a red mist. Rage. The need to destroy Fraser.

The outskirts of Princeton came into view, and he turned right onto what appeared to be the town's main street, Bridge Street. A few blocks along, he turned into a self-serve car wash, named in a small-town manner, the Bridge Street Car Wash, and rummaged in his pockets for coins to operate the machine, avoiding using his credit card. Gassing up could be explained, but washing a rental vehicle several times would be a huge red flag if the police found a reason to investigate his movements. He diligently sprayed under the undercarriage, the wheel wells, front and back, and when the time ran out, inserted more coins to repeat the process. He scrubbed the nitrile gloves, running them under the high-pressure spray before burying them deeply in a garbage can. He swallowed hard, realizing he had to check the drain covering for telltale chunks, and casually squatted down to search under the vehicle.

Nothing. Not trusting his first assessment, he got in the vehicle and moved it a few feet ahead, then acted like he had dropped something and rechecked the drain.

Still nothing. Okay, time to move on.

Refueled with gas and a large coffee, he continued south toward the community of Hope. The dark, winding highway had deer crossing caution signs every few kilometers, and on the outskirts of Manning Park, more signs warned of meandering moose. Driving carefully and at the posted speed, he kept a watchful eye out for foraging animals. Hitting an animal would damage the vehicle, causing him and the animal serious injuries and drawing the attention of the police highway patrol. He needed to stay anonymous. Just another guy—traveling on his own.

At Hope, he found a second coin-operated car wash and repeated his thorough cleaning of the underside of the Jeep and wheel wells. He swished the sprayer over the cab and windows to give the appearance that he was washing the entire vehicle, not just the undercarriage.

Topping up the gas tank, he used the restroom and bought another large coffee and two plain donuts. He had no appetite for food but recognized that he had to keep his energy level up and his mind sharp. Merging onto the busy Trans-Canada highway that funneled traffic into the Lower Mainland's continuous sprawl of sixteen large municipalities, he settled in for the final leg of the drive.

It had been at least ten years since he had driven in British Columbia, and he'd forgotten the shortcuts he'd once used to navigate the interconnected mass of three million residents. Punching the Vancouver International Airport as his destination, he let Google Maps lead the way. A few miles before the airport, he turned into a third coin-operated car wash. He didn't have any coins left, but since he was gassing up to return the vehicle, he could say he thought he was obligated to fuel and wash the Jeep before dropping it off. It was a plausible reason, maybe.

He still had to come up with a good story for his sudden trip to the Okanagan. His marketing company did business with several large firms in the Vancouver area, but he didn't have any Okanagan accounts yet. Perhaps it was time to add one or two to his list, or at least attempt. That could help explain his sudden interest in the area.

The dashboard clock changed to midnight as he drove into the rental vehicle drop-off at the Vancouver International Airport, parked the Jeep, and tossed the keys and the rental contract into the drop box. Thank God he didn't have to hang around for someone to inspect the vehicle. Hopefully, the morning car jockey would be relieved to see a clean vehicle with a full tank and assume it was ready for the next customer. With

Crushed

any luck at all, no one would notice the cracked cowling.

He checked in at the Fairmont Hotel, adjoining the airport. The room rate was pricey, but the location was convenient for his early flight to Toronto. He'd hole up in his room, order some food and a drink and try to catch a couple of hours of sleep. He chewed the inside of his cheek, then dashed to the bathroom, barely raising the toilet seat before he noisily puked into the bowl.

Fraser deserved to die.

Chapter 19

Penticton RCMP Station

Tuning out the background chatter of her workmates, Caitlin adopted her favorite position for reviewing evidence. She leaned back in her chair and rested her boots on the desk while she contemplated the whiteboard, listing the known details of their investigation: their boss, Sgt. William Williams wanted more evidence before they charged Fraser with vehicular manslaughter. Her desk phone rang, and she reached across the desk with one eye on the board and snagged the handset, "Cpl. Smith, GIS."

"Hi Caitlin, this is Trev Reynolds from the Keremeos detachment."

"Hey, Trev, what's new with you?" Reynolds was a good guy to work with, calm and thorough. The Keremeos members covered a vast area of ranches, farms, and wineries extending from the U.S. border west to Princeton and north to Penticton. Even though they worked in separate municipalities, both communities were encompassed in the South Okanagan Similkameen Detachment. They were governed by the same 'top cop,' the Superintendent, meaning her boss was also his boss.

"I have a dead body that might interest you," Reynolds cheerfully replied.

"Who?"

"Alan Fraser, the semi driver that crashed into the cyclists a few days ago."

"Was he involved in another accident?" Caitlin dreaded the answer would be yes, and that Fraser had injured or killed someone else. When forced to release a suspect because of insufficient evidence, her biggest fear was that the person would reoffend.

"No, not unless you consider him being run over several times as an accident."

"Say what?" she jerked upright in the chair, "Trev, I'm going to put you on speaker."

"Sure," Reynolds agreed.

She raised her voice, "Jones, Garcha, come here," she shouted over the clatter of conversations and ringing telephones. "Trevor," Caitlin said, "constables Ethan Jones and Natalie Garcha have joined us."

"Hi, this is Trevor Reynolds from the Keremeos detachment," Reynolds said, identifying himself to the others.

"Hi, this is Natalie Garcha."

"And Ethan Jones."

"As I told Caitlin, we have a link between your deceased cyclists and a recent murder in Olalla," Reynolds stated. "Someone went to Alan Fraser's house and, according to the evidence, waited until he came home, then ran him over before he got as far as his front porch. Repeatedly."

"Holy shit," Jones muttered.

"Ouch, someone was annoyed," Natalie added.

"We searched his house and found a substantial quantity of drugs hidden under the floorboards in his bedroom, so maybe he was behind on payments to his supplier," Reynolds suggested.

"Is he a known drug dealer?" Jones asked.

"Small time, but yes, a dealer," Reynolds answered.

"Or, it could have been James Sinclair," Caitlin said. "He's devastated by the death of his wife and daughter, and he's hitting the booze really hard."

"At this point, that's just as probable as our theory," Reynolds said. "Our coroner thinks the vehicle was high off the ground, like a truck or maybe a Jeep. If it was a car, he would have different injuries from being shoved forward on the gravel driveway and dragged by the undercarriage.

Fraser has injuries consistent with a higher vehicle driving back and forth over his inert body."

"Any additional information on the vehicle?" Jones asked.

"We've recovered a few white paint chips from Fraser's body. What type and color of vehicle does Sinclair drive?"

"He drives a big Dodge Ram, but it's dark blue, not white, and his deceased wife drove a sporty red Mazda 3," Jones replied.

"So, not likely that either of those vehicles were used to kill Fraser," Reynolds said.

"Do you have photos of the tire tracks?" Garcha asked.

"Yes. I'll email them to you as soon as we finish this phone call."

"Did the traffic investigator indicate if the vehicle had dual rear axles?" Natalie asked.

"Good question," Caitlin said. "Sinclair's company has two flat-deck trucks with dual rear axles."

They could hear Reynolds click a computer keyboard, "it says here single axle front and back."

"However, the company trucks are white, so we can't rule them out just yet," Jones said.

"Who reported his death?" Caitlin chewed on her bottom lip, mulling over this new information.

Crushed

"A friend went to his house. He said they were supposed to meet at the *Wrong Turn Tavern* in Keremeos for a few beers, but Fraser was a no-show."

"Did the friend try to call him?"

"He says he called repeatedly, but his calls went to voice mail. Eventually, he decided to drive to Fraser's property and check on him."

"Do you think the friend was getting antsy and needed to refresh his drug supply?" Jones asked.

"Yes. The friend is a known drug user. It's a good bet he was looking for more drugs," Reynolds replied, "and I just emailed you the file reference number for Fraser."

Caitlin's phone beeped. "Got it. Is there anything else that you can tell us?"

"Nope, that's about it for now."

"Okay, thanks for the call, Trev. We'll keep you in the loop from our end."

"Great, buy me a beer sometime."

"Will do the next time you come to the big city," she teased. With a population of 47,000 residents, Penticton was many times the size of Keremeos, but neither municipality was a big city.

Caitlin disconnected the call and looked at Jones and Garcha. "That changes things. Our case against Fraser is finished unless the boss still wants us to prove Fraser was driving recklessly when he hit the Sinclairs."

"Perhaps James and Tyler Sinclair will want to sue his estate for compensation?" Natalie asked.

"It crossed my mind," Caitlin admitted.

"I wonder if he has any assets? Does he own or rent his home and the property it sits on?"

Caitlin shook her head, "this is the first I've heard about a house, so I don't know if he owns it. His truck is leased, and it was badly damaged in the accident, so nothing of great value there," she shrugged. "I'll update the boss and see what he wants us to do next."

Chapter 20

Penticton RCMP Station

"How many times do I have to say it?" James Sinclair rested the heels of his hands on his forehead while his fingers dug into his scalp, massaging his temples. A combination of the bright lights and increased stress had given him a fierce headache. He badly needed another drink. "I didn't kill him."

"Do you remember saying to me, and I quote, 'He'd better not get off on a technicality, or I'll deal with him,'" Caitlin asked. She read her notes from her recent visit to Sinclair's home.

"Don't answer that, James," Leonard McCarthy warned.

When McCarthy announced that he was representing James Sinclair, Caitlin had suppressed an annoyed groan. The man was obnoxious, brilliant, and expensive. Sinclair and his deceased wife, Lorna, owned a vineyard and grew grapes under contract for other wineries, but according to their financials, they weren't rolling in cash, so how could James Sinclair afford McCarthy? Perhaps with financial assistance from his parents or his in-laws? Or a second mortgage on their home?

Ignoring his lawyer, Sinclair answered, "you had just told me how my wife and daughter had died," he stated forcefully. "I was hurt and angry. I didn't mean what I said."

"And yet you don't have an alibi." She sat across the table from Sinclair, closely watching his body language and facial expressions. The man was an emotional and physical wreck and still stank of excessive amounts of alcohol. He obviously hadn't curtailed his drinking.

"I told you. I was asleep. At home."

"And you said you were alone."

"Cpl. Smith, my client, has already answered this line of questioning," McCarthy stated. "Move on to something else," he flapped his hand dismissively.

"Yes! I was alone!" Sinclair shouted.

"James," McCarthy laid a warning hand on Sinclair's shoulder. "Why pay me to represent you and then ignore my advice?"

Sinclair irritably shrugged McCarthy's hand away, "I need to set the record straight. I didn't kill anyone."

"Alone, without an alibi," Caitlin said when the two men stopped arguing.

Sinclair moaned, "Tyler was out with his friends for the first time since ..." the words—*since Lorna and Camden were killed*—caught in his

Crushed

throat. Tears dripped onto the table. Caitlin moved a box of tissues closer to his hand. He pulled out several and wiped his face, and blew his nose. He added the damp tissues to the existing stack beside his hand.

Suppressing a gag, Jones made a mental note to spray the table with antibacterial cleaner when the interview was over. He flashed Caitlin a signal telling her he wanted to take over questioning Sinclair. "James," he spoke in a friendly tone. "Is it okay if I call you James?"

Sinclair briefly made eye contact with Jones. "What?"

"May I call you James?"

"Yes, it's fine."

"James, I can see how you'd want to get even with the man who harmed your wife and daughter." Jones deliberately omitted the word killed.

"Again. Don't answer that, James." McCarthy's voice rumbled out a stern warning.

"I didn't kill him," Sinclair wearily repeated. If he had to repeat his statement a thousand times to make them finally believe him, he'd do it—anything to get out of this situation and back to his son. *I'm useless as a parent.*

"James, you hired me to advise you," McCarthy stated.

Caitlin could hear the intense frustration in McCarthy's voice. She hoped that Ethan would be able to keep Sinclair talking despite the advice from his attorney. His stone-faced expression was betrayed by the nerve that twitched in his cheek.

"I appreciate your concern Leonard, but I'm fine, thank you," Sinclair said.

"James," Jones probed, "I'm sure you aren't unhappy that he's dead."

"I. Did. Not. Kill. Him." James said, stubbornly ignoring McCarthy's previous warnings.

"Can you think of anything to help us corroborate an alibi for you?" Jones asked. "Were you on the internet? Or watching a TV show? Did you talk to a neighbor?"

James leaned forward and rested his forearms on the table, making eye contact with Jones, "Cst. Jones, I have a serious drinking problem that has worsened since my wife and daughter were carelessly killed. Much to my shame, I was dead drunk and passed out by eight in the evening. I have promised and promised my son, Tyler, that I would do better, but I haven't," his voice dropped to a humiliated whisper. "I wasn't in any shape to drive my truck, much less kill a man."

"Well, you see, James, that's a big problem. We need to be able to verify your whereabouts."

"Fine," Sinclair sighed resignedly, "if you ask Tyler, I'm sure he can corroborate my story," he replied slowly.

"Why didn't you tell us sooner?" Jones asked evenly.

"If you were in my position, would you want your seventeen-year-old son to confirm that his surviving parent was comatose from alcohol by eight in the evening on a Monday night?"

Jones didn't answer Sinclair's self-loathing question. As a cop, he'd heard many infuriating stories about irresponsible parents, yet as a new dad Jones was appalled by Sinclair's behavior.

"We need to contact him immediately," Smith interjected.

Sinclair unenthusiastically repeated Tyler's cellphone digits.

"Wait here," she said. "Cpl. Smith is leaving the interview at 6:15," she added for the recorder.

James slumped in the chair, and McCarthy gave his forearm an insincere pat, "we'll get you through this, James."

Jones noted that McCarthy's tone sounded genuine, but his expression registered bland disinterest. Undoubtedly the arrogant bastard didn't appreciate his client blatantly disregarding his legal advice.

Smith opened the door, "Cpl. Smith is reentering the interview at 6:30." She pulled out the chair and sat across from James, "I've asked Tyler to come to the station and give a statement. Mr. McCarthy will be his adult representative for the interview. You may not speak to him until we have questioned him about the evening of Monday, November 21st. Understood?"

"Yes. But how is he getting here? He has a broken leg and doesn't have his driver's license yet."

"Cst. Swann has been dispatched to give Tyler a ride to and from the station."

"God damn it." Sinclair's shoulders drooped. "Our snoopy neighbors will be all over that."

"Under the circumstances, it's the best we can do, Mr. Sinclair," she stiffy replied. They had been stuck in the stuffy room for two long hours, rehashing his statement before he finally admitted that perhaps his son could vouch for him. *Suck it up, buttercup!*

Chapter 21

Penticton RCMP Station

"Hi, Tyler. I'm Cpl. Smith, and this is Cst. Jones," she said. "I stopped by your home recently, hoping to chat with you, but you were sleeping soundly."

"I know, Dad told me." His young face sagged with sadness and fear.

"You're not in trouble, Tyler, but we will record your statement," Caitlin said. "Your dad has authorized Mr. McCarthy to be your guardian during this interview. Do you understand?"

The teen swallowed nervously. "Yes, I understand." He shifted sideways, easing his left leg to the side, and propped his crutches against the table.

"Are you comfortable? Or would you like another chair to rest your leg on?"

"Another chair would help," he said.

Jones stood, scooped up a chair, and put it near Tyler. "Do you want me to lift your leg onto the chair?"

"Sure, thanks."

"How's that? All set?"

Tyler nodded listlessly.

Caitlin smiled at the teen. "Before we start, would you like a soda or a bottle of water?"

He nervously licked his lips. "Water would be good, thank you."

"I'll be right back, Jones said, returning a few minutes later with the bottle of water. He set it in front of Tyler.

"Okay, all set? Then in your own words, we would like you to tell us about the evening of Monday, November 21st. What were you doing?"

Tyler shot a glance at McCarthy, who nodded.

"Dad and I were at home. We had dinner. I wanted to hang with my buddies and play a few video games. They picked me up around 8:30."

"Let's expand on that a bit. When you say you and your dad had dinner, what did you eat?" Caitlin said, aiming to relax Tyler a little before asking the hard questions.

"Mac and cheese."

"My favorite," she fibbed, thinking about the disgusting, gluey texture of macaroni and cheese. "Did you make dinner or your dad?"

"I did," he mumbled.

"Do you usually make the meals?"

"Not usually." His shoulders sagged, "just since...you know."

"Since the accident that claimed your mother and your sister?"

"That wasn't an accident!" Tyler stated hotly.

"All right, let's say the incident," Caitlin replied. "Had your father been drinking?"

"Yeah."

"A lot?"

"Yes."

"How many drinks did he have?"

Tyler dropped his head and wiped his hand over his face, "I don't know, but he's been drinking a lot lately."

"Where does your dad sleep?"

"On the couch. He's got a pillow and a couple of blankets that he stacks on the end until he's tired enough to fall asleep."

Caitlin had seen the pillow and blankets and assumed James Sinclair could not sleep in the king bed that he had shared with his wife and could not use his daughter's room either. She had asked the question to confirm her assumption.

"Describe in more detail what you did before going out with your friends," she said.

The teen blushed and looked away.

McCarthy leaned closer and whispered in Tyler's ear.

"Tyler?" Caitlin prompted.

"My dad is a good person. He's just having trouble coping with his grief. Can't you just leave him alone?" he begged.

"I'm sorry, Tyler, but we need more details about the night of November 21st. So, what were you doing before you went out with your friends."

"Dad up-chucked his dinner. I helped him into the bathroom and cleaned him up. I put a clean t-shirt and a pair of briefs on him, then helped him onto the sofa." Tyler choked on a sob.

Shocked, Jones asked, "you cleaned up your dad even though you are on crutches?" Caitlin caught his eye and lightly shook her head, warning him to hold his criticism.

"Yeah, it took some work, but I fixed him up. My dad is a good person," he repeated.

Caitlin didn't respond to his declaration. Instead, she asked another question. "What color was the t-shirt?"

Tyler shot her a puzzled look. "Black. A plain black t-shirt."

"And what time did you return home?"

"Around midnight."

"Did your friends give you a ride both ways?"

"Yes." He grimaced and indicated his crutches. "It's too far to walk with a broken leg."

"Did you get home before or after midnight?"

"I don't know. I was playing a game at my friend's house, but I was worried about Dad, so I left."

"Why were you worried?"

Dropping his head to hide his tears, Tyler mumbled a few words.

"I'm sorry, Tyler, I couldn't hear you clearly. Could you please repeat that?"

Lifting his head, his raw pain caused Caitlin to suck in her breath involuntarily. "I was worried he might vomit again. I've heard drunk people can accidentally die from inhaling their puke," his voice wobbled.

"Yes," she agreed. "It is possible if the person is unconscious."

"He was. I should never have left him. Then he wouldn't be in this situation."

"What situation?" Caitlin asked.

"Needing me to give him an alibi, but I wasn't there for him. I was out with my friends, playing stupid video games."

"And when you returned home. How was he?" she probed.

"Alive. Snoring loudly like he does when he's been drinking heavily."

Which, Caitlin thought, seemed to be the norm for James Sinclair. "And what was he wearing?"

"T-shirt and briefs."

"The blue t-shirt?" Caitlin shrewdly asked.

"No, the black one. The shirt I helped him put on before I went out."

"How can you be sure it was the same black shirt?"

"It was one of his old favorites, with a white spot on the front. I think he splashed something like bleach on it one time. He won't throw it out because he says it's comfortable." His gaze dropped as he rambled on.

Caitlin studied Tyler for a few moments. "What vehicle do you drive?"

His dad had said he didn't have his driver's license, but maybe there was another vehicle that he used for practicing.

"I drive Dad's truck or Mom's car only when one of them has time to be my adult supervisor," he said, not noticing that he had flipped back to speaking about his mom as if she was still alive.

"What color are those vehicles?"

"Um, Dad's Dodge Ram is navy blue, and Mom's Mazda is bright red."

"What color are the vineyard trucks?" Her random questions were intended to verify Tyler's truthfulness. James Sinclair had already confirmed that the trucks were white.

Tyler looked perplexed, as if he was wondering why she was so interested in the color of the various vehicles. "They're white with the company logo on the doors."

"Do you drive either one of those vehicles?"

"No, not yet. Maybe when I have completed my probation and get my proper license," he said. "I can't drive anyway. My leg won't be healed for at least another month."

"You injured your left leg. You could still drive any vehicle with an automatic transmission." She said.

Caitlin abruptly turned to McCarthy. "We're done for now. James and Tyler can go, but they must advise us beforehand if they have any travel plans."

Watching McCarthy lead James and Tyler out of the police station, Caitlin turned to Jones. "Have we checked their vehicles to see if the tire tracks match the images that Reynolds sent us?"

"We don't have enough for a warrant, and even though neither vehicle fits the possible type of vehicle used to kill Fraser, I casually inspected both of their vehicles. No match. And no signs of blood or damage."

"How about the company trucks?"

"Again, no warrant, but I'll find a way to send an off-duty officer around to have a look-see," Jones replied. "The coroner did say Fraser was killed by a white single-axle vehicle, not a white dual-axle vehicle like the vineyard trucks."

"Yeah, I know. Just double checking our facts."

"Do you think the kid could have killed Fraser?"

Caitlin smiled ironically. "You know what I always say. Everyone is a suspect until they aren't."

Chapter 22

Summerland

Showered and shaved, wearing clean jeans and a fresh t-shirt, James Sinclair roughly folded the blankets and stacked them at the end of the sofa, adding his pillow on top. He dumped the empty bottles and beer cans into a plastic bucket, then added the dirty plates, glassware, and uneaten food. He swiped at the mess on the coffee table with a damp cloth, then scooted the crumbs into the same bin. Walking to the kitchen, he tossed the food into the garbage can, and the rag in the sink. He opened the dishwasher and added the dishes, then took the recycling to the garage. Camden could sort and return the recyclable beverage containers and keep the cash for herself.

A wave of despair hit him, Camden. His clever and wildly funny Camden. Gone.

Breathless with grief, he braced his hands on the kitchen counter and sobbed raggedly until his chest ached. He ran the tap, splashed a double handful of cool water over his face, blew his nose, and rewashed his hands.

Running a hand through his hair, he realized he needed a haircut. He wasn't ready for that yet. The barber he'd used for years knew Lorna and the kids. Tim was a kind and demonstrative man who had already phoned, expressing his shock and sympathy. If James entered his barbershop, Tim would likely give him an emotional hug, which could trigger more uncontrollable sobbing. He'd put off getting a haircut for another week. But what about the cremation service for Lorna and Camden? He'd have to wear a suit and get a haircut for that. He had to pull himself together; he couldn't leave organizing that terrible task to Tyler. He also had to ask Cpl. Smith when the funeral director could retrieve Lorna and Camden from the morgue.

His heart ached. His brain was foggy from grief and, if he was honest, from a large quantity of alcohol. Since being taken to the police station for an interview about the death of that fricking truck driver, he had tried to drink less. It was a work in progress. He had to get his shit together and return to work, but his heart wasn't in it. Lorna would be so disappointed in him. She had often said that she hoped Tyler and Camden would someday take over as co-owners of the vineyard and perhaps expand it into a proper winery. He should try to get back to work, even if only for a few hours. Maybe he could avoid the booze if he had something else to think about. Or, perhaps he'd do the company more harm, decision-making when he was plastered.

Reaching into the fridge, he grabbed another beer and popped the pull tab, guzzling half a can in two swallows. Returning to his now customary spot on the sofa, he slumped into the cushions. *How are we going to survive without the two of you?* He whispered to the empty room.

And how could he convince the police that he hadn't killed Fraser? *Thought about it? Sure. Done it? Not a chance.* He literally couldn't kill a fly, as Lorna frequently teased.

With another beer on his mind, he pushed himself upright. He noticed a bit of paper poking out from under the sofa cushion and absentmindedly reached for it. The photo of Lorna and an unfamiliar man he'd been looking at when Tyler called out to him. *Who are you?* Certainly not a brother because Lorna was an only child, and siblings wouldn't gaze at each other like lovers.

An old school friend, perhaps? But why did they look so happy? He flipped the photo and reread the inscription, *Mitchell 2007*. Staring at the bit of paper, an unpleasant doubt surfaced; Camden was born in early 2008. It was the year that bothered him the most.

Thinking, James tapped the photo against his hand, then whirled around and bounded up the stairs to their bedroom. With one hand on the door handle, he rested his forehead against the painted wood, willing himself to open it for the first time since her death. He hadn't even been able to shower in their primary bathroom, instead using the one Camden and Tyler commonly shared.

Since Lorna's death, Tyler had been the only one to enter their main bedroom. Thumping clumsily on his crutches, he had gathered a few pieces of clothing and toiletries, leaving them at the top of the stairs for James to retrieve. *I am a useless father*, James berated himself.

With a trembling hand, James pushed down on the handle and eased the door open. Catching the scent of her floral perfume, he forced himself to open the walk-in closet, searching for Lorna's box of family bits and pieces. Valentine's cards from him and the kids. Report cards. Old photos that hadn't been scanned into the computer. Anything that would give him a clue as to who this Mitchell was. He fruitlessly rummaged through the closet shelves, her dresser drawers, and even his, searching for anything that could settle his unease. Admitting defeat, he perched on the bed.

What did it matter?

Maybe Lorna had been briefly infatuated with this Mitchell, but he wasn't responsible for the death of Lorna and Camden. Alan Fraser had killed his wife and daughter, and he would like to thank whoever murdered Fraser.

A stab of fear jolted his thoughts. *Was Tyler capable of that?* He knew how to drive, and as long as he wasn't driving a vehicle with an L or an N bumper sticker indicating a learner or a newly licensed driver, he might have been able to avoid being pulled over by the police for driving without a fully-qualified adult supervisor. *Please, not Tyler.*

Crushed

Staring at the photo again, he made up his mind.

Chapter 23

Penticton RCMP Station

"Cpl. Smith, please, this is James Sinclair."

"One moment, please." Ethan Jones put the call on hold. "Caitlin, James Sinclair for you, line one."

She lifted the handset and punched the button. "Good day Mr. Sinclair. How can I help you?"

Sinclair cleared his throat as if trying to dislodge a lump, saying, "I found something I'd like to show you."

"What did you find?"

"A photo. It might be important. Should I bring it to your office?"

Caitlin countered, "I can be at your house in twenty minutes." Judging by her previous encounters with Sinclair, he was quite possibly inebriated.

Sinclair inhaled sharply, hating the thought of another visit from the police to his house, but at the same time, reluctant to enter the police station again. When he had been interviewed, he'd felt suffocated. He feared the doors would clang shut and lock, and he'd never be released. "Sure," he faltered, "that's fine."

Jones raised his eyebrows, interested in the discussion.

She disconnected the call and reached for her jacket, "he has a photo that he wants to show me."

"Of what?"

"Don't know. He's being very mysterious."

"Do you need me to come along?"

"No, I'd rather you continue investigating Alan Fraser's background. We need to figure out who hated him enough to kill him with such passion."

"Natalie is searching all the usual places. Nothing yet," Jones said. "I've checked his driving log books. He didn't keep them up to date, so there is no way of knowing how many hours he'd been driving before the accident. He was dispatched to wherever he was needed."

"When we questioned him at the hospital, he told us that he'd been busy driving for one of the bigger wineries, picking up bins in Oliver and dropping them off at a winery on the Naramata Bench," Caitlin said. "I'm sure those are quick back-and-forth trips during daylight hours."

"Yes, but I think he'd also been taking overnight trips to Yakima, Washington, for grapes."

She grabbed her keys, then turned to Ethan. "Yakima grapes? I thought the B.C. wineries had to use only B.C.-grown grapes."

"If they want a VQA designation, Vintners' Quality Alliance, then they use only B.C. grapes, but if they are making larger quantities of blended wines, they can import grapes to increase the volume."

She made a face. "Interesting. Okay, I shouldn't be long."

Her fist was raised to knock when the door swung open.

"Come in, Cpl. Smith." Dressed in clean clothes, Sinclair stepped aside to allow her to pass, then closed the door. She caught the scent of alcohol, too much for his body to process. He was well over the legal limit for driving.

He led the way to the kitchen again. "Sit, please. Would you like a cup of coffee?"

She accepted the unwanted coffee hoping he would relax a little. "Yes, thank you. With a bit of milk or whatever you have." The countertops had been wiped, and the empty food cartons were removed. He was trying, at least.

Crushed

Sinclair organized the sugar, milk, and spoons then poured the coffees and, with a shaky hand, placed one in front of Caitlin.

"Could you tell me about the photo you found, Mr. Sinclair?"

Bending slightly, he picked up the photo from an adjoining chair and set it on the table, "I was looking at our family photos, and this was tucked in behind another one."

Caitlin turned it over. "Mitchell. Is he Lorna's brother?"

"No," he choked out. "She's an only child. And as far as I know, she doesn't have any male cousins named Mitchell."

"Do you know him?"

"No, I've never met that person or seen that photo before."

"Who do you think it might be?"

"I don't know. We were married in 2002. Tyler was born in 2005, and Camden in 2008."

Caitlin studied the photo again. Lorna and the mystery man seemed to be fond of each other, but how fond? "What are you trying to tell me, Mr. Sinclair?"

"I don't know," he stood up and noisily blew his nose on a paper towel. "She looks so happy in the photo. Why hide it from me if he was just a friend?" He balled up the used paper and tossed it in the garbage can under the sink.

Caitlin flinched slightly when he slapped the cupboard door closed with a sharp bang. "Do you think this man, Mitchell, might have been your wife's lover?"

"I don't know what to think." He turned his head away, hiding his tears. "What if Camden isn't my daughter?"

Precisely what had crossed her mind when he recited his children's birth years. What if she wasn't his daughter? Did that mean another angry man was looking to avenge his daughter's death?

"May I take this photo? I'll have a copy made and return the original to you."

"Take it! I don't want it in the house. I hope my son never sees it."

"Let's not jump to conclusions, Mr. Sinclair. There could be a reasonable explanation."

"Look at her face!" He pointed at the photo in Caitlin's hand. "She's in love with him."

"But she stayed married to you, James. She must have loved you."

Shaking his head, he mumbled, "I don't know what to think. Did she still love me? Or was she just staying with me until our kids graduated high school?"

"I can't answer that for you." She tucked the photo inside a plastic evidence bag for safekeeping. "Thank you for the coffee." She stood up and pushed her chair under the table. "Mr. Sinclair, I must caution you. Don't drive. You are well over the legal limit." Her voice was calm and firm.

"I know." He slumped into a chair and gripped his head with both hands. "I won't drive."

"And yet you offered to bring the photo to my office."

He nodded. "It was a stupid idea. I didn't want another police car showing up at our home."

"Think of your son, Mr. Sinclair. He needs a parent." She stared down at him. "You need professional assistance, or at the very least, you should follow your wife's example and join Alcoholics Anonymous."

"I know."

Caitlin closed the front door, shutting the misery inside. It was a good bet that Lorna Sinclair had joined AA because her husband's habit was out of control. But James Sinclair wasn't ready to abstain from alcohol, at least not yet.

Chapter 24

Penticton RCMP Station

The day had turned wet and dreary, a typical late November day with low clouds hovering over the lake and blocking the weakening sunlight. Caitlin clumped her feet on the entrance mat, trying to dislodge the accumulated road grit. "Someday, I'm going to spend the entire winter in Mexico," she muttered.

"Say what?" Leaning back in her chair, Cst. Natalie Garcha looked up at Caitlin.

"I'm just bitching about the rain and the early sunset."

"It's not that bad. We won't get the torrential rainstorm that slammed into Vancouver yesterday."

"Why not?" She shook the excess rain from her jacket and hung it on the back of her chair.

"Most of the rain will fall before the storm arrives here, between Vancouver and Hope.

"Huh, this is my second winter here and I still hate the gray days."

"The lake influences our weather. It creates gray but milder winter days; quite a bit warmer

Crushed

than either Kamloops or Prince George," Natalie said.

Born in Oliver, a small town about halfway between Penticton and the U.S. border, Natalie was familiar with the whims of the Okanagan weather. She was one of the lucky recruits who, after her initial two-year posting as a rookie constable, had been able to transfer back to her hometown. She joined the federal police straight out of high school, was sent to the training depot in Regina, then to her first posting in the northern city of Yellowknife. The RCMP had a long-standing policy that personnel could not work on home turf. It was a precaution against favoritism or potential corruption. When her father suffered a debilitating stroke, Natalie had pled her case based on family hardship. She lived at home and helped care for her dad. Her fluency in her parents' native language of Punjabi, and English, French, and Hindi was also a benefit to her job. Many people of her ethnic background had settled in the south Okanagan, starting as farm laborers, and eventually owning orchards and vineyards.

"It's not warm enough for my blood," Caitlin grumbled.

"Why don't you head to a beach in Mexico?" Natalie asked.

"I have vacation days but no money." Caitlin plonked herself into a chair. "I have hefty mortgage payments on my townhouse."

Natalie chuckled. "At least you are building a nest egg."

"Yeah, well, we'll see how that goes. Do you have time to research something for me?"

Natalie quickly scanned the files on her desk. "Sure, there's nothing super serious in this pile. Is it to do with the two fatalities?"

"I'm not sure, could be, or it could be a distraction." Caitlin pulled the photo of Lorna Sinclair and the man labeled *Mitchell* out of the evidence bag.

"May I see?" Natalie held out her hand.

Caitlin handed the photo to her. "I'd like to find out who this guy is and his relationship with Lorna Sinclair."

"Mmmm. Good looking. How do you know there was a relationship?"

"Lorna's husband found it hidden behind another photo in a family album," Caitlin explained. "He says he doesn't know who the man is, and he's worried that his wife had been unfaithful to him."

"But how does that tie in with her death?"

"It doesn't, as far as I know," Caitlin conceded. "It's just a loose end."

"A first name and a year. Not much to go on, but I can have a go at identifying him."

"If something more important pops up, just set this aside."

"Of course. Leave it with me and I'll see what I can find," Natalie replied. She opened her laptop and logged on to her fake Facebook account. It was the best place to start, and then she would branch out into her Twitter, Instagram, and Tinder accounts which were also set up with profiles that couldn't be traced back to her. "I'll start with Lorna and her daughter Camden and see if I can find any connections to a man by the first name of Mitchell."

"I'm always amazed at how you can root around in social media and find so much information," Caitlin said. "I wouldn't have a clue where to start."

"I am a genius." Natalie grinned. "Do you know if Lorna grew up in this area? Knowing which school she attended would be helpful so I can search for the class photos. Maybe she and Mitch attended the same school."

"I don't know, but Jessica and Mike are friends with the Sinclairs. I'll ask her."

"Jessica Sanderson? Your favorite interfering snoop?" Natalie said making finger quotes.

"Yes." Caitlin laughed. "We've become good friends, despite her habit of poking her nose into official police business both here in Canada and Mexico."

"I can understand her desire to help the Mexican *policía* solve a case or two, but we are the smart ones. We know what we're doing." Natalie said with a wry grin.

"Uh-huh. And do you remember that Sparky and Jessica helped us with two cases; the murders of Kingsley Quartermain and Damien Crawford?"

"Beginner's luck."

"Right. I'll tell Jess you said that," Caitlin replied.

"Now, wait a minute. Don't tattle on me. She has occasionally brought goodies for us, and I don't want to be on her naughty list."

Caitlin punched Jessica's number and waited for her to answer. "Hey Jess, it's me, Caitlin."

"Hey yourself. What's up?" Jessica asked.

"What do you mean what's up? Can't I just call to chat?"

There was a pause, then laughter. "Ah, no, because you always want something."

"Busted," Caitlin said. "I was hoping you might know if Lorna or James grew up in this area. Or where they went to school."

"I think Lorna said she was going to her 25th reunion next summer at Pen-Hi."

"So, she went to school here, in Penticton?"

"I think so. At least, that's what it sounded like to me. Hang on. Mike's here. I'll ask him."

Caitlin could hear a muffled exchange, then Jessica was back speaking to her, "Mike heard the same thing, that it was a Pen-Hi reunion."

"Terrific. That helps a lot."

"But don't you already know who caused the accident?" Jessica's voice was puzzled and inquisitive.

"Yeah, we do. This is something else I'm working on," Caitlin deflected.

"Ah, so, you pump me for information, but you aren't going to reciprocate."

"Official police business."

"Right." Jessica snorted. "You aren't getting any more freebies from me."

"I'll buy you a meal at the Cannery."

"For both Mike and me?"

"Yes. For both of you," Caitlin said, then added, "you're a pain in the ass."

"Yes, I am. Tell me when you're available, and I'll check my calendar."

"I like your dog, Sparky, better than you," Caitlin retorted and disconnected. She glanced up and saw a big grin on Natalie's face.

"Really? That's the best insult you could come up with?" Natalie asked.

Caitlin rested her middle finger alongside her nose and tipped a mocking look at Natalie. She punched the numbers for Trev Reynolds at the Keremeos RCMP detachment. "Hey Trev, this is Caitlin Smith."

"Hi, you got something new on Alan Fraser?" Reynolds answered via the hands-free phone in his car.

"We've just started to investigate another angle on his murder." Caitlin watched Jones as he came around the corner of her desk with a file in his hand, and she mouthed 'later' when he gave her a questioning look.

"What's that?" Reynolds asked.

"The deceased's husband found a photo of his wife Lorna with her arm around a man named Mitchell. Sinclair says he has no idea who the guy is," Caitlin said. "In the photo, they look happy and relaxed, like they're a couple. Sinclair is worried that his wife had an affair with this man, but he has no proof."

"Is Mitchell the first or last name?"

"First. No last name. The date 2007 is written on the back."

"What are your thoughts?"

Crushed

"The daughter Camden was born in 2008, so *maybe* she's his child?" Caitlin said, unsure if this was a real lead or a distraction.

"And Fraser was a revenge killing?" Reynolds asked.

"Could be," she tentatively acknowledged, "or it could be nothing."

"Okay. Can you keep me in the loop on your mystery man?"

"Yep, will do," Caitlin disconnected and turned to Jones. "Sorry, I just got back from visiting Sinclair. That was the photo he wanted to show me."

Examining the photo, Jones waved off her explanation. "Have we found anything on this guy?"

"Nope," Natalie replied. "I've been cruising social media for any connections between Lorna, her friends, and this Mitchell, but nothing yet."

"Teachers? Coaches? After-school activities?" Asked Caitlin.

"I'm making my way through anything I can find."

"Where did Lorna work before they started the vineyard?" Jones asked, scrutinizing the photo. "I'm wondering if he was a work crush."

"A what?" Caitlin asked.

"Someone she worked with, maybe fooled around with, but didn't follow up on because she was married and already had three-year-old Tyler at home," he shrugged.

Caitlin studied her co-worker's face. His explanation seemed very specific, as if he had the same experience, yet he and Meaghan appeared to be devoted to each other and their young son, Rowan.

"I'll let you know as soon as I find anything," Natalie promised.

Chapter 25

Cannery Brewing Penticton

Jessica pulled open the heavy entrance door and walked through, keeping her hand on the door to prevent it from closing on Mike's face.

The industrial-style interior of the brewery taproom appealed to Jessica. Polished concrete floors, high ceilings with exposed pipes and ductwork painted black, and a service counter constructed of stacked river rocks caged by a wire mesh and topped with more polished concrete. The food and beverage menus were displayed on small and readily changeable chalkboard signs, listing the current selections of beers, local wines, and delicious food.

"Hi, how many?" A pleasant young man greeted them.

"Three, but our friend is already here," she pointed at the corner table where Caitlin had settled with a view of the front door and her back to the wall. *Typical. A view of everything and protecting her back.*

"Hey, Mike, it's good to see you," Caitlin smiled and lifted a hand in greeting.

"You too, it's been a while since we've seen you," he started to lean in for a hug, then changed his mind. The COVID-19 crisis changed how people greeted each other, plus she was on duty and wearing her sidearm. A public hug was a bit unprofessional. He settled for a nod and sat across from her.

"Oh, I've seen this pain in the butt a few times." She pointed at Jessica. "But I've missed your smiling face," she sweetly said to him.

"Who're you calling a pain in the butt?" Jessica retorted.

Caitlin turned her head, studying Jessica, "if the *foo shits* wear it."

"Huh, you're paying, so I'm going to order the most expensive thing on the menu," Jessica said.

Glancing at the modest prices on menu board, Caitlin shrugged. "Be my guest."

"And a glass of red wine," Jessica added, holding her hands a foot apart, "a huge glass of wine."

"Only if you aren't driving." Caitlin reached into her pocket and waggled her RCMP badge at her friend.

"Mike's driving."

"Are you?" Caitlin turned her attention to him.

"Yes, ma'am. I'm driving," Mike promptly agreed.

"All right then, I'll get you a big glass of wine. Or is that whine with an H?" Caitlin pulled herself to her feet. "Mike, what can I get you?"

"You can't trick me, officer. I just said I'm driving.'"

She laughed. "The law allows you one six-ounce drink. What would you like?"

"Honestly, a bottle of water would be great. I might have a beer with my meal."

A few minutes later, Caitlin returned to the table with three drinks and sat down, "thanks for the bit of info that Lorna Sinclair graduated from Pen-Hi."

"You're welcome," he replied.

"What are you working on?" Jessica probed.

"I told you, it's confidential. Official police business," Caitlin replied. "I'm going to order. Have you decided what you want? I need to get back to work soon."

Reading the menu board, Mike said, "that braised chuck sando sounds interesting."

A peppy tune played through the speakers, and Jessica's fingers tapped the table in time to the beat. "I'm torn between that and the crispy pork belly steam buns," she said.

"We could order both and share," Mike suggested.

"Sounds good."

"I'm going to have the pork," Caitlin said. Walking over to the cashier, she placed their orders, and as she returned to the table, the server arrived with bags of freshly made spicy popcorn, cutlery, and napkins.

"We're still waiting on the prosecutor to advise us of when we might be called as witnesses," Mike said. "I don't suppose you have any information on that, do you?"

"Which trial?" She pulled open the paper bag and shoved a handful of the warm popcorn into her mouth.

"Katherine Crawford's trial," Jessica clarified. "We got a phone call yesterday from the prosecutor's clerk, telling us we don't have to give evidence for Rodney Newcomb's trial. He's pled guilty to second-degree homicide, and his wife Louise got off with a suspended sentence for being an accomplice. You remember she provided evidence to help you charge him with murder."

"Yep, I remember, but I didn't know he'd pled out." Using her phone, Caitlin quickly made a note to check on the outcome of Newcomb's trial. "I've never had two witnesses poking their noses into multiple murder cases," she said, tucking her phone away. "It's no wonder you can't keep track of when and where you are testifying."

Mike smiled. He knew Caitlin was winding Jessica up.

"Maybe Mike and I should become licensed private investigators and help the police solve their cases," Jessica suggested.

"I think you mean Sparky should be a licensed private investigator, and you could be his go-between," Caitlin rejoined. "His emissary."

"Sparky could do a smell-o-vision identification of your perp," Jessica deadpanned. "His nose is his greatest asset for solving murders."

Caitlin laughed. "So how would that work? I'd line up a bunch of off-duty cops and my suspect, and Sparky would pick out the bad guy?"

"Exactly. That's sort of how he identified Rodney Newcomb."

"How do you figure that?" Caitlin asked.

"Oh, come on, you remember." When Caitlin didn't respond, Jessica continued, "Mike, Sparky, and I arrived at No Regrets Winery right when Ellen Taylor found the body of Quartermain. Sparky spent several minutes sniffing around the murder scene until Cst. Evan Swan kicked us out. He claimed Sparky was contaminating the evidence. A few days later, Sparky and I visited Mike at the winery. Mike introduced me to the group of directors in town for the annual shareholders' dinner."

Jessica paused, took a sip of wine, and continued her recap. "Sparky took great interest in Rodney's shoes. When we returned to our hotel, I remembered Rodney and his wife Louise arguing. She'd thrown something from his car. So, on a whim, I let Sparky wander freely, and he zeroed in on the items Louise had tossed, Rodney's prescription antidepressants," she explained. "Therefore, ta-da, Sparky identified the suspect."

"That was a long-winded rebuttal, and I concede." Caitlin chuckled. "To answer your earlier question, Mike, I don't know when you are scheduled to testify. I'll check with the prosecutor's office and let you know."

"Thanks, I'd appreciate that," he said.

"We've moved to a guest house at the winery," Jessica said. "It's a gorgeous two-bedroom cottage. You should come for dinner. If you drink too much, you can stay overnight."

"Lucky you, living in the middle of a vineyard. As for the dinner invite. Mike, are you cooking?"

"Of course," he said.

"Then I accept. Have your people call my people and set up a date."

"I could make something with my new air fryer," Jessica said. Judging by her grin, she was obviously pleased with her new purchase.

"Have you used it yet?" Caitlin asked.

"Not yet."

"Just owning an air-fryer doesn't mean that you will ever use it," Caitlin said, knowing that her cooking skills were marginally better than Jessica's. Neither of them could be bothered to research recipes and learn a few skills beyond the basics. Ordering in was Caitlin's specialty.

"It will probably join the slow cooker that's tucked into the deep dark recesses of the cupboard," Mike quipped, then ducked as Jessica took a poke at him.

Caitlin leaned back as the server placed her food down on the table. "Smells great."

"Enjoy."

"Thank you," Caitlin said to the server, then looked at Jessica. "Weren't you supposed to go back to Isla Mujeres at the beginning of November for some event or other?"

"Yes, November 1st for my goddaughter Guadalupe Yanire Maria Mendoza Medina's first birthday and baptism," Jessica replied.

"That's a mouthful for a baby's name." Caitlin said.

"It's traditional in Mexico to have several names. Guadalupe is her patron saint. Yanire to honor our friend who lost her battle with cancer. Maria for both Yasmin's mother and grandmother, and the last names of both parents. The family calls her Yani." Jessica picked up one of the pork buns and bit into it. "Oh, this is so good," she mumbled.

"Mine's good too. Here try some," Mike divvied up a portion of his meal and added it to Jessica's plate.

Her hands occupied, she pointed at her plate with an elbow. "Thanks, help yourself to mine."

"Why didn't you go?" asked Caitlin. "November in Mexico has to be better than November in Canada."

Jessica wiped her hands and sipped the wine. "It's complicated."

"My fault," Mike admitted, flicking an awkward glance at Jessica. "We couldn't find enough people to harvest the grapes at both wineries, On the Edge and No Regrets. The weather changed quickly from warm and sunny to below-freezing, and the crop was in danger. I begged Jessica to stay and help."

Caitlin chuckled. "Seriously? You gave up sun, sand, and tequila to freeze your butt off and pick grapes in sub-zero weather? I thought you were smarter than that." She took a bite of her food.

"It is what it is." Jessica avoided eye contact by concentrating on her food. "Yasmin and Carlos understood."

Caitlin watched their faces. There was a spark of tension when Jessica spoke about her friends on Isla Mujeres. She had stiffened, and she was avoiding Mike's gaze. They usually held hands or touched an arm or a shoulder and smiled lovingly whenever she saw them together. She'd never experienced a tight bond like theirs. She knew there had to be some give and take in any relationship, and sometimes tempers could flare, or angry words might be spoken in haste. This temporary unease between Mike and Jessica was unusual. *Well done, Caitlin. You've put your foot in the dog poop by laughing at Jessica for canceling her trip to Mexico.*

Jessica noticed Caitlin studying her and quickly changed the subject, "you've been holding out on us. This morning's online news posted an article about the murder of Alan Fraser." She took another bite of the pork bun, licking the corner of her mouth to catch the escaping sauce.

Caitlin nodded. "It's true. He was killed shortly after he was released from the hospital."

"Wasn't he in custody?" Mike asked. He speared a piece of his food and aimed the fork toward his mouth.

"We brought him in for a formal statement, under caution, and we released him under the prosecutor's advice pending further developments," Caitlin said. "The prosecutor didn't think we had enough evidence to charge him with vehicular manslaughter yet. Now he won't stand trial for the deaths of the Sinclair women."

"That's got to be difficult for James and Tyler to accept," Mike said.

"Any idea who killed him?" Jessica asked.

Her eyebrows twitched at Jessica's persistent questions, and Caitlin gave her the official response. "We are pursuing other leads."

Jessica pointed a finger at Caitlin. "It's someone that knew Lorna, right? That's why you wanted to know where she went to school."

"Jesus, Jess, keep your voice down," Caitlin warned.

"Sorry, sorry. You know I love to solve mysteries."

"And you'll get my ass in a sling if you start blabbing your theories around town."

"I won't say anything. I'm right, though, aren't I?"

Ignoring Mike's grin, she looked right at Jessica and reiterated. "Pursuing other leads."

Chapter 26

On the Edge Winery

Sitting on the bed, Mike removed his shoes and tucked them under his night table, ensuring that neither he nor Sparky would stumble over them in the dark. Sparky liked to sleep on the floor beside Mike, but only after his habitual fifteen minutes of cuddling with them on the bed. Undressing, Mike stacked his clothes on a nearby chair and pulled a clean t-shirt over his head. Briefs and a comfy t-shirt, his winter version of pajamas that usually only stayed on long enough to warm his skin. He loved spooning skin on skin with Jess, frequently leading to more athletic activities.

He heard the shower running and watched her remove her clothes. Folding her jeans, she placed them on her side of the bathroom counter to wear the next day again and tossed her shirt and lingerie in the laundry basket. "Got room for one more?" he asked with a hopeful grin.

She turned and half-smiled at him. "Maybe tomorrow?"

Mike sighed. Ever since Caitlin had mentioned Isla Mujeres, Jess hadn't been her bubbly and enthusiastic self. "Sweetie, I know you're disappointed about not returning to Isla for

Crushed

Yani's baptism and birthday party, and I appreciate that you stayed to help. I was desperate."

"No problem, I know you were short-handed, and harvest was rushed because of the weather change." She tested the water temperature with her hand, then stepped inside the enclosure, ending their chat.

I was married before I met you, my love, and when a partner says it's no problem, it usually means it's a big problem. He got up, padded barefoot into the kitchen, and opened a bottle of Ruby Blues Black Stiletto. Pouring a decent measure into two long-stemmed glasses, he ambled back to the bedroom and set them on his night table.

He waited until she had showered, brushed her teeth, and done whatever else she needed to do before joining him in bed. Then he handed her a glass. "We need to talk." He mentally cringed as he said those four words. In his experience, when a partner said, '*We need to talk*," it usually prefaced a difficult discussion such as I'm leaving you for another person, or my mother is coming to live with us, or I have an incurable illness.

"About what?"

"You're unhappy. Angry. Pissed at me. Pick one. Please. Talk to me."

Jessica deliberately took a sip of wine and savored the complex flavors before answering.

"Yes, I'm unhappy. Not angry. Not pissed off, just unhappy. Yasmin and Carlos are my closest friends who have stuck by me through all my many adventures and misadventures. I hated disappointing them for such an important event in their lives."

"But you told me they understood."

"I was being polite." She sighed. "As I said to Caitlin, it's complicated."

He reached for her hand, rubbing his thumb across her palm. "Then tell me."

"The Mexican culture places a tremendous emphasis on family." Setting her glass on her night table, she shifted to look directly at Mike. "As my island brother Diego Avalos once told me, family is number one, the church is number two, friends are number three, and work is number four," she said, lifting a finger with each point she made.

"But surely they understand that you and I have contracts with two wineries to perform our jobs to the best of our abilities?" Mike asked.

She waggled her hand, gesturing, *más o menos,* more or less. "You have to look at it from their point of view. Gringos, which used to mean Americans and now seems to include any non-Mexican person, are typically more focused on amassing stuff; more money, a bigger house, a more expensive car, or nicer clothes. Would you agree with that?"

Mike grinned. "*Más o menos,*" he said, imitating her hand gesture.

She smiled at his attempt to lighten her mood. "Okay, so that's our world. In their world, family comes first."

"And if a birthday party conflicts with work? Then what?"

"Then you move heaven and earth to attend the birthday party and to fulfill your work obligations. Maybe a friend can cover your shift. Maybe you talk to the boss and figure out a compromise," she said. "That's what Carlos and Yasmin would have done if our situations were reversed. They would have been there for me."

Mike reached for her hand. "Honestly, Jess, I had no idea how important it was for you to be there."

She exhaled noisily. "I've disappointed many more of my friends than just Yasmin and Carlos. Both sets of grandparents, plus Diego, Cristina, Pedro, and Maricruz, are all unhappy with me."

Mike grimaced. "How can we fix this?"

"We can't fix it," she said. "They'll forgive me, but I'll be teased and tormented for years. I'll forever be the uncaring Gringa Auntie who was supposed to be Yani's godmother but didn't show up for the baptism, and now another friend is her godmother."

"Oh, hell. I'm so sorry."

"It was my choice to stay. I could have told you no, but I love you more than any other human being and didn't want to disappoint you."

He drew her into a gentle kiss, then pulled back. "But do you love me more than Sparky?" A questioning frown bunched his eyebrows together over his hazel-green eyes.

"Jackass!" She cuffed his shoulder and then tumbled on top of him, kissing him passionately.

Mike mumbled from under Jessica's lips, "Sparky, you'd better cover your eyes and ears, bud. This is going to get X-rated."

"How is he supposed to do that? His front paws can only cover one or the other."

"He's got two perfectly useable back paws."

Her genuine laughter was a relief for his worried heart.

Chapter 27

Penticton RCMP Station

Caitlin toyed with her cell phone, turning it repeatedly in her hand. They were stuck, unable to identify the person who had murdered Alan Fraser, and Jessica's idea of using Sparky to identify a suspect was beginning to appeal to her. They would need to find a suspect before Sparky could confirm—possibly confirm—the person's culpability, and to do that, Sparky would need a scent to reference.

Was this even possible?

She pushed a hand through her collar-length red hair. Sparky had identified Rodney Newcomb as the potential killer of Quartermain. Sparky had been interested in Newcomb's shoes, and then later, he located the discarded prescription bottles, which, fortunately for the purpose of the arrest warrant, were clearly labeled with Newcomb's name. *So, sort of the same thing.*

Checking the weather app, the forecast was for rain or snow at higher elevations, which meant if she was going to do this, it had to be done now before the precipitation diluted the remaining evidence.

She punched Jessica's number and waited for her to answer. "Hey Jess, it's me."

"What's up?"

"Again, can't I just call to say hi?"

"Ah, no, because you don't."

"Whatever. It's Sparky that I want to speak to anyway."

"I'm his go-between, remember?"

"Fine, ask him if he would be interested in sniffing around our murder scene in Olalla."

"One minute, please," Jessica responded in her best imitation of a secretarial voice. "Mr. Sparky, would you be interested in helping Cpl. Smith solve another murder? What's that? You would, but this time you want to be properly compensated?"

Jessica could hear Caitlin's laughter. "Ask him what he considers to be proper compensation.

"How would you like to be paid?" Jessica asked. "Yes, yes, I understand." She said, then spoke directly to Caitlin. "He says a medium-sized bag of good quality dried liver treats would be sufficient payment."

"Agreed. Where would I find them?"

"Any good pet store, not the discount department stores."

"Fine. Are Sparky and his driver available now?"

"Yes, that can be arranged. Where should we meet you?"

"Do you know the community of Olalla?"

"I've driven through it dozens of times, but I've never actually stopped. I have noticed that interesting junk store right on the highway."

"*Zack's Town Trader*," Caitlin said. "Can you meet me in front of the store in an hour?"

"If we leave right now."

"Okay, great, then I'll lead you the rest of the way to Fraser's house."

"Can I assume that things are somewhat cleaned up?" Jessica tentatively asked. She'd never met Alan Fraser, so his death didn't have the same emotional impact as being hands-on with Lorna and Camden Sinclair. Her sleep patterns were still irregular and troubled, and she didn't need a graphic reminder of the result of a vehicle colliding with a human.

"Yes, but I want Sparky to sniff the area where Fraser was run down before the scent disappears and inside the house."

"Makes sense. I'll just tell Mike what's happening and then head out."

"Thanks."

Chapter 28

Olalla

An hour and ten minutes later, Jessica swung the car onto the gravel in front of the weirdly fascinating store that featured an eclectic mix of antiques, junk, and memorabilia. She parked behind Caitlin's cruiser and got out. "Wait here bud. I'll be right back," she said to Sparky.

Caitlin powered down her window. Jessica said, "The Sparkinator is reporting for detective duty, ma'am."

"Follow me, and park where I do when we get to the house. I don't want our vehicles to disturb the remaining evidence."

"Yes, ma'am," Jessica snapped her heels together and saluted, then walked back to her car.

Caitlin rolled her eyes and put the car in drive. She pulled away, checking in her rearview mirror that Jessica was following. She turned right onto a narrow road with a sign nailed to a Ponderosa pine. *Sorry Mr. Fraser, but your private road isn't private under these circumstances.* She parked the cruiser a distance back from the house

Crushed

and stepped out, pointing to where she wanted Jessica to park.

"Okay, so where do you want him?" Jessica asked, opening the back door for Sparky. "And do you want him on a leash?"

"Just let him wander around this area and over there where we think the suspect hid his vehicle until Fraser came home." She pointed at the churned-up dirt near the front porch and an area in the orchard. "When he's had a good sniff around here, I'll open the front door and let him check inside the house."

"What are you hoping to find?"

"I'm grasping at straws," Caitlin admitted. "If he recognizes the person's scent from the murder scene, maybe Sparky will be able to identify the killer if, and at this point, it's a big if, we find a suspect."

"I knew it!" Jessica bent and ruffled Sparky's ears. "She needs us, bud."

"Don't let this go to your head. He hasn't done anything yet."

Jessica ignored Caitlin's withering comment. "*Buscar*, Sparky, *buscar*,"

"What does that mean?"

"It's Spanish for search. I used that command when he located the pirate's treasure on Isla Mujeres."

Crushed

"I doubt you'll find treasure here," Caitlin said, a bemused expression on her face as she took in the ramshackle appearance of the small farm.

"I know, but I'm telling him this is a job."

The two women watched silently as Sparky slowly skimmed his nose over the ground, intently inhaling scents like a vacuum cleaner with legs. He walked at an excruciatingly deliberate pace to where Fraser had been run down.

"Why does he amble so slowly?" Caitlin asked.

"It gives him a chance to read and remember the scent," Jessica said.

"I thought it was just an odd habit. I've seen his painfully slow progress from your living area to his water dish in the bathroom."

"He has three water bowls, one in each bathroom and one in the laundry room, and he cautiously stalks all of them."

"Why?"

"No clue. It's just something that he does."

The women fell silent, watching as he spent several minutes inhaling the smells, before backtracking to the location where Fraser's assailant had squatted beside his vehicle, according to the techs. Next, Sparky moved to the stairs leading to the porch, then the porch deck. He carefully examined the metal oddments and discarded appliances before adding a squirt of urine to the rusty pile.

"Oops. I guess he shouldn't have done that." Jessica said.

"It doesn't matter. The FIS techs have already gathered whatever evidence they could find."

In front of the door, Sparky turned and looked at Jessica, wagging his tail. "I think he wants to go inside."

Caitlin took Fraser's house keys out of the evidence bag and opened the front door. "In you go," she said as she pushed the door open for Sparky.

The interior décor shouted that a single man lived here, a man who didn't care what his residence looked like as long as he had a roof over his head, a fridge for his beer, and a bed to crash in for a few hours of sleep. Caitlin opened the ancient Frigidaire appliance; beer, ketchup, mayo, a dried-out package of cheap cheese slices, some sliced mystery meat, and a partial loaf of bread. The staples of a life lived alone. At least her fridge contained a few fresh items and, admittedly, several cartons of half-eaten take-out orders.

"I don't think Door Dash or Skip the Dishes make food deliveries to this address," Caitlin spoke over her shoulder to Jessica. She closed the fridge door and let her eyes roam over the house's interior, taking stock.

A history of neglect could be read in the scratches, cracks, and gouges of the inexpensive fir flooring. The tattered kitchen linoleum was a pattern popular in the 1950s. Faded blue paint, worn away in areas touched by hands, covered homemade plywood cabinets containing a few mismatched dishes, a two-egg frying pan, and one battered pot. The faint November sunlight struggled to push through the dust-caked windows. It was hard to imagine that this bleak place might have once been a happy family home.

"God, this is depressing," Caitlin muttered.

Jessica did a quick one-eighty look. "A little paint, a little molding, and it would be as good as new."

"Seriously? You think this place could be resurrected?"

"A little paint, a little molding is my mom's expression whenever she and dad tackle another place to renovate and sell." Jessica laughed. "Even she might have doubts about fixing this one up."

"Speaking of your mom, any plans for your family to visit you now that you live in a two-bedroom cottage in a vineyard?" Caitlin probed. Jessica had recently told her that she had two handsome, Viking-sized brothers. Jake and Matt were in their mid to late thirties, Caitlin's preferred age range for men.

"Mom hasn't mentioned anything, but you never know, or maybe one of my knucklehead brothers will pop up for a quick visit."

"Did you tell me that Jake is the blue-eyed blonde like your mom, and Matt is the hazel-eyed ginger, like your dad?"

"Yep."

"And which one is in a serious relationship?"

Jessica smirked and didn't answer. Instead, she pointed at Sparky. "He's on the trail of an interesting scent," she said, following him into the bedroom. "Whatcha got, bud?" Sparky pawed at the rumpled mat and stuck his nose into an open space under the floor.

"He's probably following Fraser's scent. That's where we found his stash of drugs," Caitlin confirmed.

"Sparky focused on this spot pretty quickly." Jessica turned and looked back at the front door and the invisible scent track that Sparky had followed. "Maybe the killer came inside looking for Fraser?"

Caitlin grew thoughtful. "Or maybe he was looking for the drugs and heard Fraser's vehicle coming up the road. No, that doesn't work. According to our techs, the evidence suggests that the assailant waited in the orchard," she said, snapping several photos with her phone.

"Then wouldn't he have taken the drugs before killing Fraser?"

Caitlin studied the hidey hole, and the photo of the man she knew as Mitchell popped into her thoughts. "The killer could have planted the drugs to incriminate Fraser. Because we had to let him go … and he didn't want Fraser to get away with killing Lorna and Camden."

"Wow, that's an oddly specific scenario. Is that something the police teach you in detective school?"

"Detective school?" Caitlin scoffed dismissively. "There's no such thing. I just thought of it while looking at the evidence, or," she added, "maybe it's the plot from a Netflix murder mystery." And yet, she thought there was a slim chance that her theory was correct. "We have to find Mitchell," she mumbled.

"Who's Mitchell."

Damn Jessica and her sharp hearing. "No one," Caitlin hastily backtracked.

"Oh, I think he's someone, all right. I think he's a guy she knew from school."

"What are you talking about? Do you know something?"

"Only that you are very interested in Lorna's history, her school, her friends. And someone named Mitchell."

"Official police business, keep your nose out of it."

"You say that a lot," Jessica replied.

"And yet you never listen to me."

"Keep trying. Maybe one day I'll pay attention."

"I've seen enough." Caitlin pointed at the door. "Let's go," she said.

Jessica patted her leg. "Come on, pooch, Cranky Caitlin is annoyed with us, well, me, not you. She likes you." Jessica said, then bent to give Sparky a butt scratch.

"You do have a way of getting on my nerves," Caitlin agreed, shutting the door.

"Kind of like that guy at the winery a few days ago," Jessica said to herself.

Mildly curious, Caitlin asked. "What guy?"

"A guy who was downright rude."

"And what did you say to set him off?"

"See, that right there," Jessica said as she descended the few stairs leading from the porch to the driveway. "You assume it was my fault that he was obnoxious."

Crushed

"I know from personal experience you can be very annoying." Her eyes searching for missed clues, Caitlin followed Jessica and Sparky, walking toward their vehicles. "What did he say?"

"He demanded to see Dr. Crawford. I apologized and said Dr. Crawford wasn't feeling well and didn't want visitors. He got downright nasty and swore at me in a language that sounded like Russian." She nodded her head. "Huh, I just realized. It did sound like Russian. Weird."

"Just a tourist visiting our local wineries."

"Except no one in the group was particularly interested in the wine. On the other hand, he demanded a tour of the property and demanded to see Dr. Crawford." Her eyebrows pinched together as she envisioned the encounter with the unpleasant man. "He was acting as if he was entitled to explore the winery. I wonder why?"

Caitlin's cop antennae twitched. "Describe him."

"Now you want more information from me," Jessica teased as she aimed the remote at her car and unlocked the doors. She had instinctively and unnecessarily locked her car. There wasn't another living soul within sight of this remote location.

"Cut the crap, Jessica. Describe him."

Startled at the sudden aggression in Caitlin's voice, Jessica thought a moment before answering. "Mid-fifties, medium height, short dark hair going to gray, stocky but not fat, no beard or mustache. Nothing distinctive except his rotten attitude and his eyebrows. His huge black eyebrows. Like two fuzzy caterpillars glued to his face."

Caitlin thumbed her phone, flicking through work emails dating back a few months. Finding the one she wanted, she turned the screen so Jessica could see the attached photo. "Is this him?" she asked, studying Jessica's face.

Taking the phone from Caitlin's hands, she studied the image. "Yep, that's him. Who is he?"

"Mikhail Volkov. He's part of the Russian mafia. A nasty loan shark who is also into drugs, prostitution, money laundering, and pretty much anything illegal that you can name," Caitlin said.

"Is this the guy that Katherine Crawford got tangled up with?"

"Yes."

"Oh shit."

"Oh shit, indeed." Caitlin made a note in her phone. *Why was Volkov in the Okanagan?*

Chapter 29

On the Edge Winery

"I kid you not, Mike. That's what Caitlin said when she showed me his photo. The guy who demanded to see Dr. Crawford and have a tour of the winery is none other than the dirtbag Mikhail Volkov who is *allegedly* responsible for the death of Damien Crawford," Jessica said, pacing nervously. "And I say allegedly," she continued, sarcastically gesturing air quotes, "because according to Caitlin, Ivan Petrov was murdered shortly after he killed Damien, conveniently severing the link between himself and his boss Volkov."

"What does she think the Crawfords can do to protect themselves?" Crouched beside a pump transferring a red wine from the fermentation tank, Mike straightened slowly to the sound of his knees noisily reminding him that someday he'd be facing a replacement or two. In his twenties, he'd dramatically smashed his new Mustang into a semi-trailer hidden in the fog. The car was a write-off. His knees weren't much better. They had been forcefully jammed under the dashboard, damaging the cartilage.

"Honestly? I don't know. She's worried about the Crawfords, but since there isn't enough evidence to arrest Volkov, at this point, he can go anywhere he likes."

"Can the Crawfords get a restraining order?" he asked, keeping a watchful eye on his task.

She grimaced. "Does that ever work?"

"No, you're right. Restraining orders only work for somewhat law-abiding people." He huffed in exasperation. "Fricking Katherine. She's the gift that keeps on taking."

"Yep, she puts me off the idea of having kids," Jessica muttered as her phone buzzed.

Busy answering her phone, she didn't notice the odd mix of expressions scrolling across Mike's face. Relief. Sadness. Uncertainty. He still hadn't figured out if he did or didn't want a family. He was forty and thought youngsters would be harder to cope with this late in life. It was a conversation that they had so far avoided.

Jessica ended the call and turned to Mike. "That was Caitlin. She would like us to help again."

"Surely she doesn't want you involved with this Volkov guy?"

"No. She wants us to attend the cremation service for Lorna and Camden."

"We should probably go anyway, but why would Caitlin specifically ask us to be there?" Mike gave her a perplexed look. He lifted a clipboard and jotted a few notes about the wine that was being transferred.

"Because we know the Sinclairs," Jessica leaned against a sturdy metal rack holding red wine slumbering to maturity, snuggled in expensive oak barrels. She propped one foot on a horizontal support.

"I wouldn't say we are close friends, more like business acquaintances," he said. "Still, it would be kind to show our support for James and Tyler."

"Caitlin also wants us to take Sparky."

"That's an odd request. I doubt that he'd be allowed inside the building." He caught the look on her face. "What aren't you telling me?" He put the clipboard back on its hook and rechecked the liquid flowing through the pump.

"Remember our lunch at the Cannery when I reminded Caitlin that Sparky had shown interest in Rodney Newcomb's shoes and that had helped them solve the murder of Quartermain?"

"Yeah."

"She's hoping he can do that again."

"Seriously, Jess? She wants Sparky to smell the shoes of the mourners. That's insensitive," he said heatedly.

"Let me explain. When Caitlin asked me to take Sparky to Alan Fraser's home, it was to preload his memory with Fraser's scent, and possibly the killer's scent as well, and," she said, with a slight shrug, "maybe from a bunch of other people because we really don't know how many visitors Fraser had."

He nodded, waiting.

"Caitlin wants to do a test to see if he can match a scent left at the murder scene to someone at the funeral home. She suggested that after the service, I could get Sparky out of the car and hang around outside because people usually stop and chat with friends. Or if there is an interment at the graveyard, Sparky can amble around and smell stuff. I'll keep him on his leash and follow him around," she said.

Annoyed with the idea of Sparky examining the mourners for a murderer, Mike asked an irrelevant question to deflect his irritation. "Lorna and Camden are being cremated, so why would there be another service at the cemetery?"

"I don't know if James and Tyler plan to scatter the ashes later at a special place or store them in that big wall with the little niches at the cemetery. I think it's called a columbarium, and the niches are for storing urns or ashes. Either way, we should be flexible and go with the flow."

Mike crossed his arms over his chest. "You don't have a problem with this?" he asked in a flat voice.

"I do, a little," she admitted, "but if Sparky can help identify the killer, wouldn't that be a relief to the Sinclairs?"

"I don't think so," he said, his eyebrows bunching in disagreement. "The mystery person isn't the one who killed Lorna and Camden. The mystery person murdered Alan Fraser, the truck driver that caused the fatal accident. James might want to give that person a medal."

The enthusiasm drained from her face. "Oh shit, you're right."

"And what if the only shoes that Sparky zeros in on belong to James or Tyler? Then he's potentially identified one of the remaining family members as the culprit," he said. "Then what?"

She blew out a long breath. "Damned if I know." Wandering outside onto the crush pad, she punched Caitlin's number, waiting for her to answer.

"Hi, Caitlin. Do you have a minute?"

"Sure, I'm doing my least favorite job, writing a status update on the Sinclair and Fraser cases for the boss. What's up?"

"Er, this is a bit awkward," Jessica said. "I'm not keen on taking Sparky to the celebration of life for Lorna and Camden."

"Why?"

"It feels insensitive."

"But he might be able to identify a suspect."

"Or, he could wrongly identify an innocent person."

Caitlin glanced around the office and lowered her voice. "Hang on a minute, I'm going to take this outside," she said.

Jessica could hear her movements as she got up from her desk, walked past conversations between officers or perhaps phone calls, and then she heard traffic noises as Caitlin exited the building.

"So, as I was saying," Caitlin continued, "Sparky might confirm the identity of our suspect."

"You have a suspect? You never mentioned that."

"I can't share everything," she snapped. "You are a civilian, not a police officer."

"Fine, I get that," Jessica retorted. "But yes or no, do you already have a suspect in mind?"

"Why is that so important to you?"

"What if Sparky only shows interest in either James or Tyler? It would be heartbreaking if my pooch pointed an accusing paw in their direction."

"Let me put your mind at ease. We are not currently interested in either of the Sinclair men as viable suspects for the death of Alan Fraser. We have confirmed their alibis," Caitlin said. "Now, will you bring Sparky to the service?" She tried to keep the exasperation out of her voice but could feel her frustration rising. They needed a break in this case.

Using the toe of her boot Jessica pensively pushed an empty wine box off to one side of the crush pad, then changed her mind and bent to pick it up. It belonged inside, not out in the weather.

"Jess?" Caitlin asked, "will you bring Sparky?"

"Yes," she reluctantly agreed.

"Good. I'll see you there."

"Shouldn't you avoid being seen with Sparky and me?"

"We're friends. It would look odd if I ignored you. I'll say hello, and then chat with other people."

"Fine."

"I'm just trying to confirm that we are investigating the right person," Caitlin said, massaging the truth. She had a person in mind that she wanted to investigate more fully, but since they still didn't know the man's last name or his connection to Lorna, Sarge said that she needed more evidence before he'd authorize the additional expense.

"And, Jess, can you and Mike keep this between us?" Caitlin said. She was keeping her plan quiet for the moment to avoid the relentless banter of the workplace comedians. If her idea worked, terrific. If it didn't, no one had to know.

"Yep. We'll see you there," Jessica said, then disconnected. Mike stood at the entrance, listening to her end of the phone call.

"So, you're taking Sparky?" he asked.

"Yes. Caitlin says she has a suspect, but it's not either one of the Sinclairs. So, I agreed."

"Your dog, your decision." He turned and walked back inside the winery.

Okay...he's not a happy camper. Jessica carefully folded the flaps and added the empty box to the stack used by the wineshop salespeople when customers purchased multiple bottles. *I hope Caitlin's idea doesn't blow up in my face.*

Chapter 30

Funeral Chapel Penticton

Jessica's attention wandered, waiting for the service to begin. She scanned the crowd noting several familiar faces who had been at Damien Crawford's service just a few months before. As Mike had mentioned, it was a tight-knit industry, and when disaster struck, owners helped other owners, sharing staff, equipment, and supplies when needed and providing emotional support.

She squirmed uncomfortably on the hard chair. Mike was quiet, silently opposing the idea of Sparky sniffing the mourners. Attending a celebration of life was never a pleasant experience, and when one of the deceased was a teenager, it was doubly difficult. *How do families survive the death of a child?*

An unfamiliar man sitting at the back caught her attention. He was wearing a ballcap inside the chapel. That would have been considered rude a few years ago, but who knew what the rules were now? *Was he Fraser's killer?* The person would probably be a man, but that wasn't guaranteed. The killer had used a truck or something similar to run over Fraser several times, which didn't require muscles. Rage and the willpower to commit the act would be more important than physical strength. So, at this point, anyone with a driver's license was a suspect. She continued scrutinizing the crowd.

If the killing was about drugs, then perhaps the police were concentrating on his known associates. Sitting on an uncomfortable chair in a cheerless room filled with melancholy people, she couldn't spot anyone who looked like a murdering drug dealer. *Was there a specific type of person to fit that job description?* She'd had a dangerous encounter with a Cancún drug lord, and unless you were up close and could see the lack of empathy in his dark brown eyes, he looked like a thirty-something, muscular Latino sporting a bushy mustache. Again, what does a murderer look like?

If the killing was to avenge the deaths of Lorna and Camden, then the person was more likely a family member or close friend—someone who passionately cared for one or both women. Caitlin had admitted that James and Tyler had strong alibis, but what about the others? The chapel's front row was occupied by two sets of parents who looked to be in their mid-sixties, plus James, Tyler, and another woman. Lorna was an only child, so perhaps the woman was a sibling of James? Would the woman, or her partner, be capable of driving a vehicle over Fraser? Either one of the fathers would have a reason to kill and use a vehicle as a weapon. Either one would be physically able. I wonder if Caitlin checked their alibis?

Jessica turned to the right, searching for Caitlin, and spotted her standing at the back. Her eyes were also scanning the crowd, hunting. *Great minds and all that. Maybe I should have been a cop.* Since asking which school Lorna had graduated from, Caitlin hadn't accidentally dropped any more helpful hints about their case.

Mike softly cleared his throat, and she swung her gaze to the front, then snuck a sideways look. He met her eye and lightly squeezed her hand.

Sorry, she mouthed with a guilty smile.

Mike rolled his eyes at her. That translated to—you're being a meddlesome snoop.

When the service ended, Jessica whispered to Mike, "I'll get Sparky and see you outside."

He grunted in agreement.

She moved across the aisle, then made her way along the perimeter of the room and out the front door to their car. "Come on, Sparky, let's give you something to do," she said, opening the car door and attaching his leash. Giving him a few minutes to investigate and respond to a few pee-mails, she hustled him closer to the front entrance. Hovering nearby, she smiled and exchanged small talk with several people, all while keeping an eye on Sparky.

"He's so cute. What type of dog is he?"

"He's a Mexican low-rider," she replied.

Crushed

"A low-rider. I've never heard of that breed," a man chimed in.

"He's some sort of terrier mix. It's common in Mexico to see a dog with a long body and short legs. That's why the rescue societies refer to them as low-riders," she explained with a smile. In a world that values high-end designer dogs, people frequently asked the breed of a dog. The more costly the breed, the more social status it reaped. Her answer was her way of saying mutts were worthy of love and affection, no matter their lineage.

"Did you rescue him from Mexico?"

Not wanting to get into a lengthy explanation of how she had found Sparky on Isla Mujeres, Mexico, she took the easy route and simply replied. "Yes, he's a rescue."

"I love rescues. Did Lorna and Camden know him?" Another person asked.

"They met him once or twice," Jessica said.

"How kind of you to bring him to their celebration of life."

"Oh, he wasn't inside. He was in the car, and I just wanted to make sure he was okay," she said. "Would you excuse us? Sparky wants to greet someone he knows," she explained as Sparky leaned into his harness, directing her to follow him. She swung her head around, quickly searching for

Caitlin, and saw her intently watching Sparky's movements.

Jessica followed his lead as he slowly scanned the ground. His tail began to twirl in helicopter mode, his signal that he'd either discovered a cute girl dog he wanted to meet or had caught a scent of something interesting. *Let's hope he doesn't lead me straight into the arms of a murdering drug dealer.*

The same man she had noticed at the back of the chapel stood off to one side. Dressed in a dark suit and black overcoat, he had his plain black cap pulled low over his brow, obscuring his eyes. He tensed when he saw Jessica and Sparky walking his way, then rapidly moved toward the sidewalk. When he reached the street, he blipped the locks on a dark sedan and quickly slid behind the steering wheel. Signaling, he smoothly accelerated into traffic.

Sparky thoroughly investigated where the man had been standing, then tugged Jessica toward the curb, following the man's route to the car.

"Dammit," Caitlin muttered from behind Jessica's shoulder.

"Do you think that was him?" Jessica quietly asked. "Sparky seemed to recognize his scent."

"It's a good bet that was our guy. Judging by the photograph, he's about the right build and

Crushed

height of a man we want to interview. He's driving a rental car, but I only caught the last three digits."

"Didn't you have plainclothes officers photographing the license plates of every car near the chapel?"

"What TV program have you been watching?"

"Wait, did you say you have a photograph?" Jessica spotted two mourners watching their exchange on the sidewalk and lowered the volume on her voice. "You never said you had a photo of your suspect."

Caitlin gave Jessica an incredulous look and, leaning closer, she quietly said, "do you not understand? You are *not* a police officer." She straightened and keyed in a number on her cellphone. "This is Corporal Smith. I want a search on all cars rented in B.C. over the last week, Nissan Ultima, dark blue, new model. Partial plate, PE1. The first or last name of the client could be Mitchell." She disconnected and huffed a curse.

"Can't you put up roadblocks for the routes leading out of town?"

"On what grounds?" Caitlin's sharp tone wasn't lost on Jessica.

"You said he was a suspect."

"I have an old photograph of a man I want to question about three deceased persons. This

Crushed

man, who just departed, could be the person in the photo. Or perhaps he had an urgent appointment."

"Sparky was interested in him."

"Great, I'll tell Sergeant Williams that I need to put an APB on a suspect Sparky identified."

Jessica heard the frustration in Caitlin's voice, but she couldn't stop a retort rolling off her tongue. "And yet you wanted Sparky here to do just that. Identify your mystery man from the scent at the murder scene."

"You're right. It was my brilliant idea. And if you could keep this to yourself, I would greatly appreciate it."

"Paw Patrol," Jessica replied, smiling knowingly.

"What the hell are you talking about?"

"The first time we met while leaning over Quartermain's corpse at No Regrets Winery, I know you checked my background. You phoned a retired RCMP officer who had moved to Isla Mujeres a couple of years ago and asked about me. So, you know that Sparky and I helped the *policía,* solve a few murder cases," she said automatically using the Spanish word for police.

"And?" Caitlin impatiently rolled her hand. "What does that have to do with me?"

"Sparky and I bumped heads a few times with two Cancún State Police detectives, Marco

Cervera and Dante Toledo. They were nicknamed Patrulla de la Pata, Paw Patrol, by their coworkers because, in their opinion, Marco and Dante couldn't solve a crime without the help of Sparky," she quietly said. "And you are afraid that someone will do the same to you. Make you the target of their jokes."

Caitlin's expression changed from annoyed to concerned. "You have no idea how juvenile cop humor can sometimes be. Don't breathe a word of this."

Jessica's eyes crackled with mischief. "We can be bribed." Just loudly enough for Caitlin to hear, she whispered to Sparky. "Would you like your Auntie Caitlin to buy you a nice piece of steak?"

"Is there a gathering at the cemetery now?" Jessica asked Mike.

"No, the two families are privately scattering the ashes another day. The Crawfords have arranged a small get-together at their house."

"That's handy for us. I'll put Sparky inside the cottage and see what I can do to help."

"Did Caitlin get what she needed?" Mike asked as they walked with Sparky toward the car. "Do you want to drive, or should I?"

"You can drive." She said as she opened the rear passenger door for Sparky. "Caitlin sort of got what she needed."

"I saw the two of you whispering back and forth. You looked very conspiratorial."

"Did we? I thought we had been careful," she answered, securing her seatbelt. She checked over her left shoulder, ensuring Sparky was settled in the back.

"I don't think anyone, but me, noticed." He started the car and pulled out. "Are you going to make me ask?"

"Ask what?"

"Did Sparky identify the suspect?"

"Sort of," she hedged again. "Caitlin thinks the guy matches a photograph of someone she's interested in questioning, but he left before she could talk to him."

"So now what?"

"She's trying to find out exactly who he is through the rental car agreement," Jessica smiled at him. "Are you still annoyed that I did this for Caitlin?"

"Nope. I didn't want to upset the family, but I don't think they knew what was happening."

"Good." She looked out the window, then chuckled. "So, I have a funny thing to tell you about Caitlin, but you must promise not to say anything to anyone. Except her. You can tease the hell out of her."

Chapter 31

Penticton

"You stupid ass." Mitchell Ross berated himself. "Why did you panic like that?"

He wasn't sure what was going on with the blonde woman and her scruffy dog, but when the dog began to walk in his direction, an alert red-haired woman followed. Dressed in civilian clothes, the second woman had the no-nonsense demeanor of a cop. He'd lost his nerve and fled.

Twice the woman's watchful eyes had swept over him inside the chapel and again while he lingered outside, waiting for what, he wasn't sure. He wanted to offer his condolences to Lorna's parents, whom he'd met once or twice when he and Lorna had been high school sweethearts. It hadn't felt right to barge into their grief and try to explain why they may or may not remember him. *And by the way, Camden was my biological daughter, so that makes us family.* He sighed deeply. There was no point in further devastating the two families with that bit of unwelcome news.

Since their deaths, he'd been watching for an announcement for their celebration of life. As soon as he knew when and where, he'd made his travel arrangements. Yesterday he'd flown from Toronto to the Kelowna airport, an hour north of Penticton, to attend the service. Now, he was rushing to distance himself from the red-haired woman, cutting short his final farewell to the two women he loved.

Driving a little over the speed limit, he turned onto the Channel Parkway bypass, moving toward Kelowna. His flight wasn't until much later in the evening. *Maybe I can get an earlier flight.* Noticing a small shopping mall, he turned in and parked. Keying in the number for Air Canada reservations, he anxiously waited for the interminable messages. Press 1 if you want English. Press 2 if you want French. Press 3 if you want reservations.

"God damn it! I need to talk to a real person!" He fretted.

Frustrated, he disconnected and opened their online booking site. Bugger the cost. He'd abandon the return portion of his ticket and book the earliest available flight. The next flight to Toronto was scheduled for two-thirty. He glanced at the time; barring any traffic accidents, he could make it. He only had to drop the car at the airport lot, toss the contract and the keys in the return kiosk, and hustle inside to departures. Only business class had seats available—for the eyewatering price of nearly three thousand dollars, one way. And every single flight flew west from Kelowna to the hub of Vancouver before flying for five hours east to Toronto. Even if the first leg of the flight from Kelowna to Vancouver was uneventful, there was still a risk the police could detain him in Vancouver—if they truly were hunting him.

I'm overreacting. I should have waited to see what was going on with the dog. I can't see why the cops would be interested in me so soon. God damn it, I'm an idiot.

He sighed, removed his American Express card from his wallet, and paid for the ticket. He put the car in drive and resumed his journey north. Passing through the lakeside communities of Summerland, Peachland, and West Kelowna, he crossed the Bennett Bridge and drove through the congested city of Kelowna. Twenty minutes later, he spotted the turnoff for the airport. *So far, so good.*

Parking in the rental returns lot, Ross grabbed the rental contract out of the glove box, snatched up his overnight bag, and walked quickly toward the self-return booth. He tossed the document and keys inside the locked box and strode towards the departure gate. He'd forgotten to refuel the car, and at this point, he didn't give a damn about the extra cost. Utilizing a kiosk, he checked into the flight and proceeded to the security screening. Willing himself to stay calm, he put his overnight bag in a plastic bin and scooted it toward the scanners. At the signal from the guard, he walked through the scanner. It beeped, and

Crushed

Ross's heart rate accelerated. "I'm sorry. I completely forgot my belt," he said. "Should I remove it and try again?"

"No, raise your arms," the unsmiling guard replied, using the wand to confirm his belt bucket was the only problem. "Go ahead."

Ross thanked him and retrieved his belongings. *Relax. Relax. Don't look worried. There are surveillance cameras everywhere.* If the police had a reason to question him and ask about his sudden and expensive departure, he'd need a plausible answer. Appearing to be frightened would undermine his believability.

Family emergency? That would necessitate someone in his family lying convincingly to the police. Off the top of his head, no one who would be willing to take that risk and successfully pull it off came to mind.

Business emergency? He owned the company and could probably get away with that, except his administrative assistant was a very astute woman and not given to telling or believing bullshit lies.

Grief? He wanted to pay his respects to Lorna, but the reality hit him harder than he expected because they had been lovers when they were younger. This was closer to the truth, and it may work.

He checked the flight. On-time. Once on board, he'd have several hours to construct a credible reason for his abrupt departure.

Settled in his business class seat, he breathed a small sigh of relief. He ordered a whiskey and soda as soon as the beverage service was available. The only good thing about paying for the expensive upgrade, he was served long before the others.

Putting in earbuds, he tilted his seat back and shut his eyes. Images flicked behind his closed lids, Lorna's beautiful smile and happy laughter. That first time they had made love. A kaleidoscope of images. They had lost touch after graduating from the University of B.C., and a few years later, when his employer sent him on a business trip to the Okanagan, he had phoned her to say hi, how are you doing? She had suggested they meet for coffee at Starbucks, and when she'd walked toward him in the café, he'd fallen in love all over again. Like a moth to a flame, her smile drew him. He knew she felt it too. Within minutes it was just like old times.

"Would you like another drink, sir?"

Ross opened his eyes. "Thank you, the same again, please." He watched the flight attendant place a fresh glass with ice, a small bottle of whiskey, and a can of soda on his tray. He poured the drink and sucked in a mouthful. Leaning back, he closed his eyes and resumed daydreaming about Lorna. The pregnancy had been a shock. She said she was using contraceptives but had missed a couple of days. He had stupidly blurted out, "how do you know the baby is mine?"

Mortified, Lorna had admitted that James hadn't been interested in her sexually for quite some time. He drank himself into a stupor every night after dinner, even fifteen years ago. When she discovered that she was pregnant, she'd expressed her desire for a second child, a playmate for Tyler. At her request, James reduced his drinking and cooperated with making a baby.

By the time Camden was born, Ross was eager to step up and be a full-time dad, but Lorna begged him not to claim his daughter. To leave her family as a cohesive unit. To wait until the children had graduated from high school. Then, she promised she'd tell James that Mitchell Ross was Camden's father. To date, his only parental contributions had been to pick her name and to send money to Lorna surreptitiously. She, in turn, mailed photographs and long newsy handwritten letters about Camden. Lorna had diligently avoided emailing or phoning Ross. She was terrified an electronic trail would expose her secret.

He exhaled forcefully. *And now, my love, your caution might help me out of the mess I've created, making it more difficult for the police to find me. But it doesn't change the fact that our beautiful daughter is dead, and she never got to meet me. Not once.*

Swallowing a sob, he coughed loudly and used a paper napkin to wipe his eyes.

"Everything okay, Mr. Ross?" asked the flight attendant.

"Yes, thank you. The whiskey tickled my throat and made me cough and my eyes water," he answered with a teary smile.

"I have that same reaction, but with pickles. The vinegar makes me cough so hard people think I'm choking," she said. "And the tears, oh my goodness. Thankfully I wear waterproof mascara, or I'd have black rivers running down my cheeks." She chuckled.

"Embarrassing, isn't it?"

"A little," she admitted. "We are landing in Vancouver in a few minutes. Let me know if you need anything."

"Thank you, I will." He rolled his neck, feeling the pull of tight muscles. The next flight was five hours, still time to sort out his story for the police. As much as he'd like to think that they weren't interested in him, the stone-faced scrutiny from the red-haired woman said otherwise.

Crushed

Chapter 32

On the Edge Winery

Weaving through the crowd with a tray of canapes, Jessica quietly offered the tasty snacks to anyone that glanced in her direction. Mike was busy pouring On the Edge wines and non-alcoholic options.

The Crawfords' spacious, contemporary home featured a wall of windows with a stunning view of their vineyards that dropped off toward Okanagan Lake. How incredibly sad that neither of their children would inherit this property. Damien was dead, and Katherine was in prison waiting for her trial date.

When Danielle and Keegan purchased the property, planted the vineyard, and built the winery, Damien had enthusiastically thrown himself into learning the day-to-day operations. He had hoped to be the general manager when his parents eventually retired. His two daughters, April and Amy, were still young children and wouldn't be interested in the vineyards and winemaking until they had graduated from high school. Or perhaps by then, the dream of their grandparents and their father would not be their dream, and the winery would eventually be sold.

"Would you like another crab puff?" Jessica asked a winemaker from a nearby property.

"Thanks so much. These are so yummy," the woman said, scooping up two bite-sized morsels.

Bliss, the Crawfords' aging golden retriever, watched with drooling anticipation, hoping for a dropped morsel. Mike had warned Jessica to keep an eye on the gentle old dog. She adored food but was forbidden from eating salty or fatty foods. "I'm sorry, sweet girl. Nothing for you."

Danielle Crawford gently touched Jessica's arm, "Jess, you don't have to do this. I paid the catering company to handle everything."

Jessica leaned in and whispered. "Two of their staff were no-shows. Mike and I have it under control. Don't worry."

"Really? I had no idea."

"It's fine, Mrs. Crawford. We enjoy helping."

"Well, thank you for helping, and please, for heaven's sake, call me Danielle." A tailored black dress accented with understated gold earrings enhanced her olive-toned Mediterranean complexion.

"Thank you. Would you like a crab puff?" Jessica asked, offering the goodies.

"Maybe later," Danielle said, "I must see to our guests."

And that's how Danielle stays so beautifully slender, Jessica mused, tallying the number of savory bites that had disappeared into her own mouth.

She glanced at Mike. He had temporarily relinquished his bartending duties to Lauren Michaud, his assistant winemaker, and he was deep in conversation with Keegan Crawford. Mike was nodding in agreement with whatever was being discussed.

A few minutes later, Keegan lightly tapped a spoon against his wine glass. "May I have your attention for a few moments, please?"

It took a minute or two for everyone to stop talking and turn their attention to where Keegan stood beside Danielle, James, and Tyler. "As we all know, this has been an unbelievably tragic week for our friends. Danielle and I wish to express our condolences and support to James and Tyler for the days ahead." His vision blurred; their family situation was comparable. "We've asked James and Tyler if we could label our newest Cabernet Sauvignon in memory of Lorna and Camden." He paused and looked at James and Tyler. "They have agreed and suggested that we label it The Best of the Sinclairs."

Applause broke out, along with quiet exclamations of appreciation for the gesture. James stood mutely with his arm clenched tightly around his son's shoulders. Tyler's face was etched with emotional and physical pain while he balanced uncertainly on his crutches.

Keegan continued, "it's been a long and difficult day for James and Tyler, and they ask that you please excuse them. Your support today has been much appreciated." He knew James was barely hanging on, and Tyler was desperate to get his dad home. "Thank you again, and please stay as long as you wish."

James bolted out the door. Humiliated, Tyler started to apologize to the Crawfords, but Danielle gently wrapped the teen in her arms, and momentarily reverted to her childhood language as she comforted him. "*Non, ma chérie.* Don't worry. Take your dad home and look after him." Pulling back, she looked into his eyes. "And take good care of yourself, too," she said, pointing at his cumbersome cast.

Tyler nodded mutely and clumped toward the door.

"James," Keegan called as he followed the elder Sinclair to his car. "Our friends Paul and Ryan have offered to give you a ride home. One will drive your car, and the other will follow in their car."

"That's unnecessary," Sinclair retorted as he dug out his keys. "I'm fine."

Crushed

"It is essential, my friend. I know exactly how you are feeling. It's all arranged," Keegan gave him a fierce hug and handed the car keys to Paul. The drive from the winery in Naramata to the Sinclairs' home in Summerland was at least thirty minutes, and James was an emotional wreck. Keegan had also detected the smell of alcohol that followed James and noticed he'd consumed two or perhaps more glasses of wine in the short time he'd been inside the Crawfords' home. He was in no condition to operate a vehicle.

"Come on, Tyler," Keegan said. "Let's get you settled. There is more room for you and your bulky cast in Ryan's car."

With Keegan and Ryan's help, Tyler maneuvered his backside onto the rear seat, then, using his right leg and arms, he dragged his injured left leg inside. He gave Keegan a grateful look. "Thank you so much, Dr. Crawford, for everything."

"My pleasure, Tyler. You can call me anytime," Keegan said, pushing a business card into the teen's hand. "My cell number is on there. Call anytime. I mean it."

Turning his head away, Tyler nodded.

"I don't know if you remember." Keegan leaned inside the car and softened his voice. "My son Damien was killed a few months ago. I know too well the pain of losing someone you dearly love. So, please, call me anytime you need someone to talk to. Or, if you prefer, call my wife, Danielle. You'd be helping us too."

Unable to meet Keegan's concerned scrutiny, Tyler wiped his eyes and sniffed loudly. "Thank you, Dr. Crawford, that means a lot to me."

Chapter 33

Naramata

Heather Lapointe unlocked the door to their double-car garage for the first time since Nathan's death and flicked on the lights. She walked dispiritedly to the spot where he had fallen just a few days before, lying on the cold concrete floor, unable to help himself. If he hadn't left his cell phone in the adjacent workshop, could he have used it to call for help? By the time she'd found him, he couldn't speak or move one side of his body.

She heaved out a long sigh. Why hadn't she brought Nathan a coffee just a little sooner? Perhaps he'd still be alive. Even then, he might have survived the stroke if that big truck hadn't struck the cyclists, overturned, and completely blocked the road. The local news outlets reported the truck driver, Alan Fraser, had been killed shortly after the accident. The police weren't saying if his murder was related to the deaths of the Sinclair women or to his suspected drug dealing.

She sympathized with the Sinclair family who had lost both a mother and a daughter in the crash, but they were strangers, and their grief wasn't as present and overwhelming as her personal anguish. So many families damaged by one horrific accident.

Nathan was gone, and she was rattling around in a too-large house for one person. No children, no pets, just her. Nodding decisively, she spoke aloud. "To hell with waiting a year before making a big decision. I'm going to list the house with a real estate agent tomorrow."

"Sis? Are you in there?"

"Yes, I'm here," Heather replied, still eyeing the stack of furniture.

Her older sister, Taylor, stepped inside and crossed her arms over her thin chest. "Damn, it's cold in here."

"Yes, I suppose it is chilly," Heather answered, still lost in her thoughts.

"Mom's been asking where you are," Taylor said. "So, what are you doing out here?"

"Just wondering what I'm going to do with all of this stuff." In truth, she didn't know why she had come out to the garage. Perhaps because, for two days, the house had been claustrophobically jammed with grieving relatives who constantly pushed her to eat, sleep, sit, or do whatever *they* thought would soften her grief.

"Mom is really worried about you, sis. Could you come back inside?"

Crushed

Heather turned to her older sister and smiled weakly, "I will, Tay. Just give me another minute or two. Okay? I can't listen to Mom's endless advice right now." Her mother's world-class ability to fret over her children could take weeks to talk down from its spiraling heights. She meant well. She couldn't accept that her babies were adults capable of resolving their own problems.

Taylor's face betrayed her indecision. Even as a child, her parents had tasked her to keep track of her three younger siblings, and yet, they were all adults whose children were nearly adults. She crossed the few feet separating them and hugged her sister tightly. "Take your time. I'll figure out an excuse to keep Mom happy."

"Thank you, sis, I really appreciate it," Heather said, giving Taylor another affectionate squeeze before releasing her hold.

The garage door closed, leaving Heather in solitude. She surveyed the stack of tables; large, small, round, square, and rectangular. Comfortable deck chairs designed for summertime evenings. Decoratively carved boxes to hold keepsakes and personal treasures. Nathan had carefully crafted all the items using high-quality wood that had been sanded and varnished until pieces were satiny smooth to the touch.

Tears rolled down her cheeks as she hunted for a tissue or even a piece of paper towel in the clutter of his creations. He had a solid and loyal customer base, and his designs sold well at the local craft fairs. A part of her resented the hours and hours he spent in pursuit of his solitary pleasure; another part was proud of his artistic ability.

"What am I going to do with all of this stuff?" She kicked at a small end table; it toppled over and struck the concrete. The loud and oddly satisfying noise ignited a flurry of rage and grief in her heart. She attacked the stack of furniture, bracing both arms against a table and heaving it over like a helpless turtle lying on its back. One leg cracked. She tossed an ornately carved box across the width of the garage, striking the far wall with a splintering crash.

"Why? Why? Why? God damn it, Nathan, why did you die?" she bellowed, beating an armchair with a broom until the wooden handle cracked in half.

"And God damn you Alan Fraser! This is all your fault and I'm glad you're dead," she screamed. "I hope you rot in hell!" The damaged broom fell from her hands as she slid down a wall and landed on the floor, barely noticing the cold concrete pressing against her legs.

"Why you, Nathan?" she whimpered. "Why you? I'm too young to be a widow!"

Time passed. Her teeth chattering from the cold, she slowly rolled onto her knees and stiffly pulled herself upright. Without a backward glance at the destruction, she turned off the lights and slammed the garage door shut. The thought of selling the furniture to recoup some of their money was unbearable. How could she stand for hours at a craft fair with a stiff smile plastered on her face, extolling the virtues of her dead husband's artistry while potential buyers haggled for a better deal? *Not going to happen.*

She strode into the house and ignored the questioning glances. Perhaps they had heard her screaming outrage but chose to let her vent. Or maybe her disheveled appearance and scuffed hands made them uncomfortable, worried she was on the verge of a psychotic meltdown.

A glass of wine was pressed into her hand, followed by a gentle kiss on her head. "I love you, baby girl," her dad's gruff voice said. This man would quietly ignore the temporary insanity of his daughter, the grieving widow.

"I love you too, Daddy." Squeezing the wineglass with enough force to make it creak ominously in her hand, she slumped against her father. His once muscular chest felt frail and bony where she rested her head. "Please, Dad, stay with us for many, many, more years," she whispered.

"Don't you worry. I'm not going anywhere, sweetheart," he said. Catching his wife's eye, he held up a cautionary hand, telling her to stay where she was and let their daughter relax.

Chapter 34

Penticton

After the funeral Caitlin returned to the station to hunt for the unknown man who had rapidly driven away from the funeral home. She didn't attend the gathering at On the Edge winery. Several of the group knew she was a police officer, and they might be uncomfortable with the idea that she was scrutinizing the families and studying the guests. To be fair, she was trained to analyze people in every situation.

"Anything on the dark blue Nissan driven by our mystery man?" she asked Jones.

"Not yet," he said. "How was the celebration of life?"

She grimaced. "Sad and somber."

Jones did a quick visual check, ensuring no one was listening to their exchange, then leaned closer. "Did Sparky immediately focus on that guy?"

"Yes, and I'm sure it was the same man from the photo that Sinclair gave me. Mitchell somebody," she said. "I'm certain we're on the right track, but this waiting is so damn frustrating."

Crushed

Later in the afternoon, she tossed her pen on her desk, "I'm done," she said to Jones. "I'm going home."

"Me too," he replied, reaching for his jacket. "See you tomorrow."

"Yep, unless something changes before then." She logged out of her computer and greeted Natalie. "You're on afternoons again?"

"Yes, I asked for this shift. It works out better for my parents," Natalie replied.

Knowing Natalie's home situation, with her dad needing around-the-clock assistance, Caitlin gave the younger woman a warm, supportive smile. "Have a good shift, Nat. If you discover additional information about our mystery man, please call me. This case is driving me crazy."

"Will do. Enjoy your evening."

Caitlin grunted a chuckle, "I have an exciting dinner date with my bitchy cat."

Pouring a glass of wine, Caitlin surveyed her compact two-bedroom, two-bathroom townhouse in a quiet cul-de-sac near the middle of the city. Luckily, she had purchased it before the real estate price war of the previous spring when buyers were bidding against each other and paying well over the asking price. A recent substantial hike in mortgage

Crushed

rates had discouraged speculators, dramatically cooling the overheated market.

She purchased the thirty-year-old condo in an estate sale after the previous owner, an elderly woman, had passed away peacefully in her bed. Her agent had been worried that Caitlin would shy away from the property, but as heart-wrenching as it was for someone to die, death was inevitable for all living creatures.

"No one gets out of life alive," she said. She raised her wine glass and saluted her cat, Tickle.

Tickle was all black except for a triangular patch of white on her chest. Caitlin frequently referred to her as Tickle the Terrible, or the Evil Bitch, because she liked to slash any unsuspecting hand that dared touch her exposed and invitingly soft tummy. The cat was an ungrateful little demon that had once pooped right in the middle of the Miata's windshield because she had been accidentally locked in the garage overnight. And yet her fiercely independent nature appealed to Caitlin.

Staring at the old-fashioned kitchen cabinets, Caitlin's reoccurring fantasy to update the condo interior re-emerged. Once again, the renovation disruption, her changeable shifts, and her tight budget pushed that dream below the surface. Her home was comfortable and easy to maintain, good enough for now.

Her cell phone vibrated on the countertop, still set to silent mode for the celebration of life.

"Got him!" Natalie Garcha shouted as soon as Caitlin said hello. "His name is Robert Mitchell Ross."

"Is he our guy?" Caitlin's pulse kicked up a notch. Maybe this was the break she needed to solve the case.

"Yep. I received an email copy of a rental agreement for a dark blue Nissan and accessed his driver's license. Same guy. A little older and grayer, but it's him."

"Where does he live?"

"Toronto."

"Damnit, I doubt the boss will pay for me to fly out and interview him."

"Can't Toronto do that for us?"

"They can, but it's not the same as looking the suspect in the eye," Caitlin said. "Does he have any local connection?"

"Yes, once I knew his full name, I found him in the Pen-Hi school photos. He graduated two years ahead of Lorna, in 1996."

"But I thought you'd already searched there." She rested her hip against the counter, her head tipped sideways as she visualized the information she had written on the whiteboard.

"I did. There were two reasons I didn't find him the first time. He was Robert Ross until he graduated, then he switched to Mitchell Ross. And he missed the photo day. I only found him because of a candid shot of a basketball tournament. He was on the Pen-Hi team."

"Any idea why he changed his name?"

"Maybe he liked the sound of Mitchell or Mitch better. It's not uncommon for teenagers to suddenly dislike the name their parents gave them at birth."

"True," Caitlin agreed. "I had a friend who legally changed her first, middle, and last names. Something to do with its numerical value. I don't remember exactly what the deal was."

"Numerology?"

"Yeah, that sounds about right," Caitlin replied. "Back to Mitchell Ross. Anything else you can tell me?"

"Not yet, but I'm searching for classmates who still live in Penticton, who might know if Lorna and Mitchell were a couple."

"Judging by the photo, I think there must have been a spark between them at some point," Caitlin said. "Can you also search for vehicle rentals in the last two weeks under the name of Robert Mitchell Ross or any combination of those names?"

"To see if he was here when Fraser was killed?" Natalie asked.

"Yes," Caitlin said, "he's worried about something. Sparky spooked him today."

"Sorry? You lost me."

"What?" Caitlin realized that she'd spoken inadvertently out loud about Sparky, focusing on her suspect. "Oh, sorry, I'm just rambling."

"Okay. I'm here until midnight," Natalie said. "If I find anything significant, I'll call. Otherwise, I'll leave a report on your desk."

"Thanks." Caitlin disconnected the call and addressed her SPCA rescue cat, comfortably sprawled on a kitchen chair cushion. "That calls for another glass of wine. Wouldn't you agree, Tickle?" The cat slowly blinked once, then scornfully raised a back leg, and began to groom her private parts meticulously. Playing the cello, as her mother would say.

Opening the fridge, Caitlin removed the Indian and Chinese take-out remains from the previous two days. Or was it longer? Giving the containers a sniff, she decided that the food smelled acceptable and dumped everything onto one plate, then microwaved it for ninety seconds.

Hearing the microwave ding, Tickle meowed and jumped down.

Crushed

"Are you hungry?" Caitlin asked, reaching into the cupboard for a tin of Fancy Feast. Scooping a tablespoon onto a small saucer, she added some of the cat's ridiculously expensive, veterinary-prescribed kibble and set it on the floor. Tickle sniffed, lashed her tail from side to side, and sat down with a mulish expression.

"Trust me, princess, that's all there is." Caitlin carried her food and wine to the table, "I don't do pet catering. Maybe you should move in with Jessica and Sparky. He gets roasted chicken or sometimes steak with his dinner," she taunted her offended cat.

Looking down at the mangled assortment of food on her plate, Caitlin could hear her mother's voice, *presentation is everything, dear.* Reaching for a placemat and colorful napkin, she asked, "there, are you happy now, Mom?" *When did she last video chat with her parents? A month ago? Two months?* "I'm a horrible daughter," she said, bringing a forkful of food to her mouth.

Rapidly chewing her food with little awareness of the flavors, she scrolled through her social media updates, noting an upcoming event, the winter wine festival at the end of January. It might be fun to go if she could find a couple of available friends. She bookmarked the date and continued scrolling.

On her second mouthful, it hit her. "I wonder if James Sinclair is a local boy?" she asked her disinterested cat, "Mitchell Ross went to Pen-Hi, so maybe they crossed paths at some point. But then why would James deny knowing Mitchell?"

Chapter 35

Penticton

Quickly setting her fork on her plate, she called Natalie Garcha. "Hey Nat, it's me again. Did James Sinclair grow up here? Did he go to school in Penticton or Summerland?" she asked, rapidly accessing her mental spreadsheet of unanswered questions.

"I don't know. I haven't searched that deeply into his background."

"My mistake. I should have thought of it sooner," Caitlin admitted. As the lead detective, it was her mistake. She'd let herself get sidetracked with proving Fraser was at fault in the death of the Sinclair women and had forgotten to dig deeper into James Sinclair's personal history. On the surface, he appeared to be a grieving husband, and father, with an out-of-control alcohol problem. But was his drinking as bad as he had led her to believe? Could he have killed Fraser? Or was the photo a misdirection to protect someone else, perhaps Tyler?

"What are you thinking?"

"James denies knowing Mitchell Ross. What if he does know him? Then that changes a few things."

"Like what?"

"Maybe he purposefully gave me the photo to waste our time focusing on the wrong person," Caitlin said.

"We checked Sinclair's alibi for the night of Alan Fraser's murder."

"The alibi was given by his teenage son Tyler, who admitted that he was out for part of the evening playing video games with a friend. What if Sinclair was faking and wasn't as drunk as he pretended to be?" she asked. "Maybe Tyler was accustomed to seeing his dad drunk and unconscious by early evening, and he believed his dad was incapable of driving."

"Good point. Okay, I'll investigate Sinclair's background more thoroughly after I search for rentals in the name of Robert Ross or Mitchell Ross."

"I'll be up for a while yet. If you find anything interesting, call me."

"Will do."

Caitlin poked at her cooling meal and shrugged. "It'll fill the hole," she said, then aimed her fork at Tickle. "You ungrateful little brat, eat yours, or I will," she threatened.

With a flick of her tail, the cat strutted away, giving Caitlin a clear view of the five-pointed star adorning the spot where her tail connected with her body. It was the cat equivalent of a one-finger salute.

Checking the time, Caitlin shook her head in disbelief, "did I really just watch four hours of *The Last Kingdom*?" she asked Tickle. The cat stretched, yawned, and resettled comfortably, with her tail covering her nose. She was ready for bed. Caitlin's phone chimed, and she checked the message; call me if you are still awake. Natalie. She punched the numbers. "Hi, Nat, what's up?"

"Did I wake you?"

"Not a chance. I just spent four hours watching a loose historical interpretation of the period when the Danes, the Scots, and the Brits battled for control of the various kingdoms in Britain. Lots of gory battles, thousands killed, and every episode had a steamy sex scene, so I am wide awake now," she said.

"I wouldn't be able to sleep either after watching something like that," Natalie said. "I was going to email you, but a phone call is quicker."

"Did you find out more about Ross? And Sinclair?"

"Yes, to both. James Sinclair first," Natalie said. "He grew up in Vancouver and dated Lorna when they were both at UBC. They married in

2002, then lived and worked in the Lower Mainland. In 2005, they moved to Summerland and purchased a 1940s farmhouse on ten acres."

"Is that the property on Morrison Drive?" Asked Caitlin.

"Yes, that's the one. Lorna has worked for the Royal Bank for many years and was promoted several times. James concentrated on renovating their home and starting the vineyard. They sell their grapes to local wineries, like On the Edge, where Mike Lyons works."

"Interesting, I didn't know there was a connection between the Sinclairs and the Crawfords."

"The wine industry has many interconnections and close relationships," Natalie said, "like the orchardists."

Natalie spoke from experience. Until recently, her parents had owned an apple orchard in Oliver. When her dad suffered a debilitating stroke, they were forced to sell the property and move into a one-level home designed to accommodate his wheelchair.

"Okay, so James Sinclair didn't go to school in Penticton, and he might not know Ross," Caitlin summarized. "What can you tell me about Mitchell Ross? Did he recently rent a truck vehicle in B.C.?"

"Hang on a minute. There's more background," Natalie laughed lightly. She had spent hours researching these people and wasn't about to rush through her report, "Mitchell Ross attended UBC at the same time both Lorna and James were enrolled."

"Now that is very interesting. Did they share any classes?" Caitlin asked. "I know it's a longshot because the UBC Vancouver campus is massive, something like 60,000 students. But maybe they met there."

"Possibly. I'll dig further tomorrow. Mitchell was there from 1996 until 2001. Both James and Mitchell obtained an MBA in Business Management. Lorna graduated with a Bachelor of Arts."

"What about the vehicle rental? What did you find out?"

"Ross rented a vehicle for five days," Natalie paused deliberately, like an imaginary drum roll before an important announcement. "He rented a white Jeep, the Rubicon model.

"What dates?" Anticipation coursing through her nerves, Caitlin unconsciously crossed her fingers.

"His rental contract was for Saturday, November 19th until Wednesday, November 23rd, except he returned it to the Vancouver airport very early on the morning of the 22nd."

"*You* are a goddess, Natalie Garcha," Caitlin loudly exclaimed. Tickle raised her head and gave her a filthy glare for disturbing her sleep. Caitlin stuck out her tongue at the cat, relieved that no one else had witnessed the brief juvenile exchange.

Natalie laughed. "I thought you would like that bit of info. I'll print this and leave it on your desk."

"Thanks so much. Chat tomorrow." Setting her phone down, she eyed her empty wine glass and had a brief tussle with herself. *A third glass? No, not a good idea.* She would need a clear head in the morning. Her first task would be to brief Jones on the newest development and then plead her case with Sarge for a trip to Toronto to interview Mitchell Ross.

Chapter 36

Penticton RCMP Station

Caitlin rapped her knuckles on the door frame.

"Enter," Williams said without lifting his eyes from the spreadsheet on his computer monitor. Budget constraints. Staff shortages. And monthly targets. It was all a massive pain in his too-large ass. Years ago, when he'd been promoted to Staff-Sergeant, he'd been excited for the pay raise to help with the escalating cost of raising grocery-devouring teenagers. Now their two sons were adults with little ones, and he was a middle-aged grampa who sorely missed the excitement of taking down the bad guys.

"Good morning, Sarge. I've brought you a large double-double," Caitlin said, setting the Tim Hortons coffee on his desk, "two creams and two sugars." Jones followed her inside the office and stood to one side, his feet comfortably braced and his hands tucked behind his back.

Williams removed his glasses and massaged the bridge of his nose with his forefinger and thumb. His optometrist had recently changed his prescription to progressive lenses to accommodate everything from reading the computer screen to driving. The change was another sign of the passing years. He was still having difficulties adjusting to the various strengths of the complex lenses, stumbling like an old man over his size twelve shoes.

He deliberately pushed the coffee cup with one finger, moving it a couple of inches away as if he was rejecting her bribe, "what do you want, Cpl. Smith?"

"Can't I buy my favorite boss a cup of his favorite coffee?" Smiling brightly, she pointed at the chairs, "may we sit, Sarge?"

He didn't answer. Instead, he turned his flat-eyed stare on Jones. "What's she up to, Cst. Jones?"

Resisting the urge to grin, Jones shifted his feet and kept quiet.

Williams swung his glare back to Caitlin, "what do you want?" he repeated.

"May we sit, boss?" With an even wider smile, she again indicated the chairs.

"If you must." He picked up the cup, removed the top, and gingerly tested the temperature with a tiny sip before inhaling a satisfying mouthful. Too many times, he'd burned the roof of his mouth on scalding hot coffee, and the resulting blisters made eating and drinking uncomfortable for several days. Expressionless, Williams swallowed a second mouthful. "I don't have all day," he said. In truth, he enjoyed sparring with Caitlin. When she'd first transferred to the Penticton detachment, she had been intimidated by him until she realized that his bark was worse than his bite, and yet when he did bite, it hurt like hell. With experience, she'd discovered how to stay clear of his snapping jaws remaining respectful yet fearless.

Caitlin spoke succinctly, presenting her information in verbal bullet points. "We've had a break in the Fraser case. We've identified a man who was a close friend of Lorna Sinclair before she married James Sinclair. His name is Robert Mitchell Ross. All three attended UBC at approximately the same time. We believe he was here in the Okanagan when Fraser was murdered. That has yet to be confirmed, but we're working on it. I saw Ross at the celebration of life for the Sinclair women. He left suddenly when he noticed my interest in him," she did not mention that Sparky had also taken a keen interest in Mitchell Ross. She didn't want that piece of information known unless it was unavoidable. Either way, it could wait until they'd tied up loose ends. "We have reason to believe that Ross may, in fact, be the natural father of Camden. We think that he killed Fraser in retaliation for the deaths of Lorna and Camden Sinclair. He lives in Toronto, and we'd like to interview him personally."

Jones silently nodded in support of her assessment. When Caitlin briefed him on Natalie's new information, they had agreed that Sarge wouldn't authorize two officers to fly to Toronto because of budget constraints. They planned to suggest they both go, knowing Williams would whittle it back to Caitlin. It was one of those win-win situations that self-proclaimed experts prattled on about. Jones had little interest in leaving his wife and son alone for a rush trip to Toronto. Caitlin could easily handle it.

"We have these things called phones," Williams pointed at the black multi-line device sitting near his right hand. "I'm pretty sure Toronto has them too." Blanking his face, he drank more coffee, waiting to see what her next move would be.

"Yes, Sarge, but as you have said, watching a suspect's body language and facial expressions is far more effective than a phone call," she argued.

Quoting me, personal interviews are more effective than a phone call. Smart move. "What other evidence do you have?" Williams asked.

"He rented a white Jeep, in Vancouver, from November 19th to November 23rd. Fraser was run down by a white vehicle on November 21st. Ross returned the Jeep early on November 22nd and immediately flew back to Toronto."

"That's not enough. You need hard evidence that Ross was here in the Okanagan when Fraser was killed," Williams stated.

"We're working on it, boss."

"Come back when you have the proof."

"So...that's a maybe, Sarge?" she cheekily asked.

"Next time, bring chocolate chip cookies with the coffee," he said, tipping the last sip of coffee into his mouth and lobbing the empty container into the garbage can under his desk. "Close the door on your way out," he said, pointing at his rarely shut door, "I have a pile of paperwork that needs to be finished today." From under his lowered eyelids, he watched them leave, smiling at her tenacity. If they had an unmarried son, he'd be tempted to have his wife, Kyla, play matchmaker. Caitlin would be an entertaining addition to their family, someone whose eyes wouldn't glaze over when he talked shop. However, both of their sons were happily married, and he loved their wives, so there was no point in stirring the pot.

Williams minimized the report he was working on and opened his departmental budget. He might be able to massage the figures and justify an economy-class ticket and overnight expenses for one, which he was sure had been the original goal of her presentation.

Chapter 37

Penticton RCMP Station

Back at their desks, Caitlin studied the two whiteboards in the incident room. One had all the information for Lorna and Camden Sinclair, with CLOSED scrawled across the top. The other was designated for the active case of Alan Fraser's death. "We need to track Mitchell Ross's credit card receipts for November 19th to 22nd. To see what he was up to," she said to Jones as she added the information about Ross, the truck rental, and his Penticton connection.

"Too bad Natalie is on the late shift. She's a wizard at this stuff."

"We know how to do it. It's tedious but not that difficult."

"Before we get started, do you want another coffee?"

"And how long will that take?" Caitlin asked as she continued to make notes on the board.

"Starbucks is only a few blocks away."

"I know, but it's the time that you take once you are at Starbucks."

He raised his right hand in a traditional salute. "Scout's honor. I'll stay in the car, order our drinks, and come straight back. Is that okay, Mom?"

"Yep, and it's your turn to pay. I'll have my usual latte." She stepped back and examined the added information. There were still far too many holes in the timeline.

"I'm pretty sure I paid last time."

"Think of it as a partial refund of my change. The change that you habitually use as a thirty percent tip for the baristas," she reminded him. It was an ongoing battle between them, not serious, just a constant back and forth. Him: in her view, overly generous. And her: more inclined to stick to a fifteen percent tip. He was an incurable flirt, particularly at Starbucks, but anyone that knew him understood that he and Meaghan were devoted to each other and their son Rowan.

"You're a cheapskate," he objected, "I, on the other hand, like being generous to people who earn minimum wage." He shrugged into his jacket and sketched a wave in her direction.

Caitlin briefly watched Jones as he walked away. Jessica had once described him as a cross between Matt Damon and Ben Affleck, cute and trying to look tough.

"Okay," she said, tapping her computer awake, "Mr. Robert Mitchell Ross, what were you doing in B.C. when Alan Fraser was murdered?"

She was deep into credit card charges for Mitchell Ross by the time Jones returned with their drinks, "anything interesting?" he asked, setting her coffee and a pastry beside her elbow.

"Thanks," Caitlin pried the lid off and unconsciously mimicked Sarge by testing the temperature with a small sip before risking a larger mouthful. "He fueled the Jeep and bought snacks in Princeton, again in Hope, and then refueled and washed the vehicle in Richmond."

"Strange that he would need to refill the gas tank three times during a 400-kilometer drive."

"My thoughts exactly. My car will do the five-hour drive on one tank of gas."

"Your Miata weighs about as much as a hummingbird. The Jeep is heavier and would use more gas, but three fill-ups? That seems excessive."

Caitlin looked at the amounts. "The credit card charges are between twenty-five and thirty dollars. I think he was topping up the tank, not completely filling it."

"Weak bladder and had to hit the washrooms frequently?" Jones suggested.

"If he was in his sixties or older, I'd say that he probably suffers from an enlarged prostrate and had to urinate often, but a guy in his forties?"

"Stress can cause problems with your gut. If he did kill Fraser, maybe he had the runs."

Caitlin snorted a laugh. "Listen to you, Dr. Google."

"Experience. Not from killing anyone, obviously, but stress plays havoc with my guts."

"Your wedding night must have been interesting," she leaned back, giving her eyes and shoulders a rest from reading the computer screen. "The stress of the big day and then having to perform your husbandly duties."

"No stress. I was passed out cold across the hotel bed five minutes after we checked in."

"Did Meaghan want an annulment because you didn't consummate your marriage?"

"Nope, she fell asleep beside me. Our friends plied both of us with too much champagne, and by the end of the night, we had progressed to tequila shots," Jones twisted his face into a grimace. "To this day, I can't stomach the smell of tequila."

"Me too, but for a different reason," she grinned at the memory.

Jones flapped his fingers. "Come on, give. I shared an embarrassingly intimate secret with you."

"It involved a beach in Puerto Vallarta and too many traditional-style margaritas made with just tequila and fresh lime juice."

"Details."

Caitlin's laugh contained embarrassment and a touch of amazement for her foolhardy younger self. "Late one night, there was a big group of drunk guys screeching like little kids about the sea snakes coming up on the beach. I decided to show off and *save* the snakes by tossing them back into the sea. In the morning, I discovered my shorts were speckled with blood spots. Several snakes I had flung into the waves had bitten my fingers."

"Holy shit! What were you thinking?"

"That's the point. Tequila stops you from thinking," she said. "As it turns out, the yellow-bellied sea snakes are harmless. They didn't appreciate being roughly handled, and according to one local, they were trying to lay their eggs in the sand. I didn't check to see if that was true, but I've never had another margarita since, or any drink made with tequila." She drained her coffee. "Okay, let's get back at it, partner."

Jones pointed at her uneaten pastry. "Do you want that?"

"Go ahead, I'm not hungry," she said, pushing it toward him. "How do you eat so much junk and stay so thin?"

"I hit the gym four times a week, although, since the arrival of Rowan, that has dropped off dramatically," he admitted. Chomping down on the sweet treat, he remembered something Caitlin had said about the credit card charges. He sputtered a mouthful of damp crumbs on her desk as he blurted out a question. "A car wash? Why?"

"Jesus! Jones, that's disgusting! Didn't your mother train you properly?"

"Sorry, my bad," he said, quickly swallowing the remainder of the pastry. "I just remembered something you said earlier about Mitchell's credit card charges. Why did he wash a rental vehicle before returning it?"

"Why indeed." Caitlin's finger skimmed the credit card entries until she found the item on the statement. "Good catch, partner. We need that Jeep," she said excitedly. Using a piece of paper, she brushed the soggy bits toward the garbage can, pretending she didn't notice when most landed on the floor.

"Not likely that it will still have forensic evidence at this point."

"Our FIS guys are magicians. If there is a tiny bit of tissue anywhere on the chassis, in the wheel wells, or the suspension, they will find it," she looked up the car rental company's customer service phone number and began the frustrating process of trying to access a real person. She needed the vehicle's exact location before asking another detachment to retrieve it for forensic testing. And she'd need Sarge to approve the expense of seizing the vehicle. The rental company would not be happy. Their unit could be out of service for several days as FIS searched the vehicle looking for blood, hair, tissue, or bits of bone.

"Ethan, can you update the boss and get his okay to impound the Jeep? I'm on hold, waiting for a human."

"You're the senior investigator, so you should do the update. I can wait for someone to answer."

"Okay," she handed the handset to Jones. She hit print for the document on her screen and strode excitedly toward Williams' office.

Fifteen minutes later, she slid into her chair, watching Jones rapidly make notes on a piece of paper.

"Yes, that's the vehicle we are interested in," he said. "And you are sure it's still at the Richmond Airport location? Has it been rented after November 22nd?" With a triumphant grin, he gave Caitlin a thumbs-up. "We are seizing the vehicle for a few tests. Please ensure that it stays exactly where it is. An RCMP recovery vehicle will be there within an hour," Jones said, before replacing the handset. "The Jeep hasn't gone out on a rental since Mitchell Ross returned it," he excitedly explained. Then as his eyes tracked her slight nod to the left, his enthusiasm faltered and died. Sgt. Williams stood off to the side, listening intently to Jones.

"I assume you gave the okay, boss?" Jones asked tentatively.

Williams glowered at the younger man. "You'd be up shit creek about now if I hadn't, wouldn't you?"

"Yes, Sarge. Did you authorize us to impound the Jeep, boss?"

"Ask your supervisor," Williams said, pointing at Caitlin with his old, chipped mug emblazoned with World's Best Grandad. He strode in the direction of the vending machines in search of coffee. As awful as it tasted, it was still a hit of caffeine. Something to keep his brain functioning while he worked on the tedious spreadsheets. He should have sent Jones on another coffee run as penance for assuming he'd authorize the seizure of the truck. He sighed—then the union would be on his ass for mistreating his staff. *The old days were so much more entertaining.*

"Did I overstep?" Jones asked. "Or did he authorize us to seize the truck?"

"Relax. Sarge is having a bit of fun," she reassured him. "We're good to go. Why don't you call the Richmond detachment and get that in motion?"

Chapter 38

Penticton RCMP Station

"Cpl. Smith," Caitlin answered.

"This is FIS technician Alex Logan, RCMP Richmond."

"Good afternoon, Alex," she responded after a quick glance at the bottom of her computer screen to confirm that the morning had indeed morphed into late afternoon. "Do you have good news for me?"

"Preliminary news. We found some damage to the underside of the vehicle as well as a trace of tissue and several hairs. The evidence has been sent to the lab for testing. Hopefully, we've found enough for DNA analysis," he said.

"Awesome!" Unseen by Logan, Caitlin punched the air with satisfaction.

"I thought that would brighten your day. That's why I called instead of sending an email," he said.

"Did you find anything inside the Jeep?"

"No, it had been thoroughly cleaned by the rental company."

"And our suspect," she said. "He returned a clean vehicle. We have a credit card charge for gas and a car wash in Richmond on the night he dropped the Jeep off at the airport car rental parking lot."

"Topping up the gas tank is cheaper if you do it before returning a rental. But washing it? That's very unusual."

"Exactly. That's how I convinced Sarge that we needed to do a forensic search of the vehicle," Caitlin said. "At least you've found something that justifies the expense."

"Cst. Jones said you believe the vehicle was used as the murder weapon?"

"Yes. The person who rented the vehicle is currently our prime suspect. He or someone ran over our victim several times," Caitlin confirmed.

"Judging by the type of damage that I did find, the victim must have been on the ground when he was run over," Logan replied.

"We don't know for certain. The victim, Alan Fraser, was involved in a serious traffic accident two days before his death. His truck and flatbed trailer plowed into a group of cyclists. There were two fatalities, and a third person was seriously injured."

"Was Fraser injured in the crash?"

"According to the doctor, nothing serious," she replied, "although he was limping and not moving quickly after his release from the hospital. We did a formal interview with him here at the detachment."

"So, he probably couldn't outrun the vehicle," Logan stated.

"I don't think he even tried. The Jeep was hidden a short distance away, and Fraser had walked about five feet before he was struck. There's no indication that he tried to run," Caitlin explained. "What I can't figure out is why the rental company didn't notice the damage to the vehicle."

"The plastic cowling, that bit of plastic underneath the bumper, was the only obvious damage. It was cracked. No one would have had any reason to look more closely or check underneath the vehicle," Logan said. "I found a bit of tissue stuck in the crack and three hairs in the suspension." He'd spent a couple of hours lying on a shop-dolly with a bright lamp attached to his head, creeping around under the vehicle searching for anything that might be evidence.

"So no other damage to the truck?"

"A few scratches and scrapes on the underside where his body collided with the transmission and the oil pan," Logan replied. "Luckily for the driver, the airbags didn't deploy. That would be impossible to hide from the rental company."

"Even so, if the vehicle was still drivable, he could have used the old *I hit a deer* excuse, especially if he used the Hope-Princeton Highway. It's dark, winding, and overrun with deer and some moose in certain areas," Caitlin said. "Any other damage?"

"Just normal wear and tear," Logan replied.

"Thanks again, Alex. If you have any influence with the lab, please put a priority rush on the testing. We're desperate for solid evidence."

Logan laughed. "I get the same outstanding treatment that we all get—two to four weeks minimum," he said, with a touch of sarcasm.

"I hear you. It's frustrating. We have our suspect in our sights but can't bring him in without the confirmation that the Jeep was used to kill Alan Fraser."

"Keep looking. Maybe you'll find another bit of evidence that you can use to scare him into confessing."

"Thanks for the pep talk," she laughed. "Let me know if you ever need help with anything."

"Will do, bye."

Caitlin stood and twisted her shoulders, left then right, working out the kinks from intently staring too long at the computer monitor. She picked up the marker pen and added the new information to the whiteboard. Ever so slowly, they were building a case against Mitchell Ross.

None of the media outlets had picked up on their interest in Ross, partly because he lived in Toronto, and Penticton residents wouldn't be aware of the police poking into his life. James and Tyler Sinclair knew because they had been questioned about Alan Fraser's death. She was confident they wouldn't share that information because Sinclair worried that his overly interested neighbors were judging him every time a police car arrived at his home. Caitlin was confident that the name Mitchell Ross wasn't top of mind for anyone except her team and perhaps James Sinclair. He had, after all, supplied the photo that started her along this line of inquiry.

And that still puzzled her. Had Sinclair pointed the finger at Mitchell Ross out of malice? A feeling of betrayal by his wife? Or was he trying to protect himself? Or Tyler? Thinking, she drummed her fingers. Tyler's friend had confirmed they had played video games on the night of Fraser's death, but did the friend own a white truck? Annoyed at herself for not checking sooner, she added it to the whiteboard.

Stepping back, she perched her butt against a nearby desk and continued to study the information. The media had been relentless with the death of Lorna and Camden. Two well-liked, attractive local women dead. Initially, the reporters had howled like hounds at the press conferences, demanding answers. Was Alan Fraser intoxicated? Was he criminally responsible for their deaths? Question after question with scarcely enough time to answer before a competing news agency fired off another. Once the news got out that Alan Fraser was dead, the frenzy died off. A small-time drug dealer meets a violent end. It wasn't a catchy headline for television or the newspapers.

Jones reappeared after a long interval in the washroom. "Something new?" he asked when he saw she was staring intently at the board.

"The FIS tech, Alex Logan, found body tissue and hairs under the chassis. He's sent everything to the lab." She replaced the erasable marker on the skinny ledge at the bottom of the board.

"We're on the right track, finally!"

"Yep, but getting a DNA confirmation will take weeks, assuming there is enough tissue for the lab to test. The tech, Alex Logan, suggested we keep looking while we're waiting for the DNA results. Do you have any bright ideas?"

Jones grinned. "I don't suppose we can arrest Ross using Sparky's identification?"

Caitlin barked a short laugh. "Jessica calls it Sparky's smell-o-vision. He was interested in Ross at the celebration of life. Who knows, maybe Ross just had doggie treats in his pocket."

"Sparky doesn't like doggie treats," Jones said. "Only steak."

"Be careful of your adoration of the pooch." She leaned closer and quietly told Jones about the Paw Patrol moniker given to the State Police detectives in Cancún, watching his face as the realization hit him.

"Shit," he whispered hoarsely, "don't let anyone hear you say that."

"I know. I said the same thing to Jessica," Caitlin said. "She just laughed and demanded steak for Sparky as a bribe for her silence."

"If that starts, we'll never live it down," Jones said.

"At least she's stopped referring to us as *Alias Smith and Jones* from that 1970s TV western."

Chapter 39

Penticton RCMP Station

"Smith. You and Jones, in my office, now." Williams shouted as Caitlin walked past his open door.

"Will do, Sarge. Two minutes, please." She pointed towards the washrooms, hoping he understood that she urgently needed to empty her bladder.

"Two minutes," he shouted at her retreating back.

Unzipping her pants, Caitlin sat on the toilet and phoned Jones. "Sarge wants to see us ASAP."

"Where are you? It sounds echoey on the phone," he asked.

"Not that it is any of your business, but I'm taking a leak."

"You're right. TMI, too much information. I'll meet you in his office," he responded. "And don't forget to wash your germy hands."

"Yes, mommy." She put her phone away, flushed, and zipped her pants. After washing her hands, she used the paper towel to pull on the door handle, wondering yet again why the garbage can wasn't located closer to the door, or the washroom wasn't designed with a door that opened out and a handle that could be operated with an elbow. She propped the door open with one foot and stretched to stuff the used paper into the opening of the covered container. A random notion popped into her thoughts; this counted as a stretching exercise and was quickly followed by, I need to restart my gym membership.

"You wanted to see me, Sarge?" she asked, entering his office.

"Sit," Williams pointed at the two chairs opposite his.

Caitlin gave Jones a side-eyed look, wondering if he knew what the sergeant wanted. He moved his head slightly. *No clue.*

Her butt had barely touched the seat when Williams said, "your trip to Toronto has been denied."

She reflexively jerked upright as if she was about to jump to her feet. "Sarge, we need to interview Mitchell Ross personally," she objected. "He's our prime suspect." She had expected this, but she wouldn't give in easily.

Glaring at her over the top of his glasses, Williams asked, "was I not clear? Your request has been denied," he said, pushing a piece of paper in her direction. "This is your contact at the Toronto

Police Service, Detective Callum McHugh, Major Crimes Division. Call him."

"Sir, we need..." she started again.

Williams raised an authoritative hand. "Call him. He will do the preliminary interview. If the DNA testing of the tissue evidence comes back as belonging to Alan Fraser, then Robert Mitchell Ross will be detained by Toronto Police pending your arrival to take him into custody."

"That could be weeks or months."

"I am well aware of that Cpl. Smith," his hands clasped together, Williams rested his forearms on his desk.

Ignoring the warning in his voice, she retorted, "I'm owed vacation time. I'll pay my expenses, Sarge."

Williams straightened his shoulders and flicked his glare at Jones, "Cst. Jones, you're dismissed. Close the door behind you."

"Yes, boss," Jones leaped to his feet and hurried out the door.

Maintaining a neutral expression, Caitlin studied Williams. The RCMP was based on a military model, and her toe was nudging the fine line between fighting for her request and outright insubordination.

Williams turned his impassive stare back to her. "Cpl. Smith, do you want to go down this road?"

Realizing her toe had indeed slipped across the line into insubordination, she stood and adopted a respectful stance with her feet braced shoulder-width apart and her hands clasped behind her back. "I apologize, Sgt. Williams, I'm frustrated," maintaining a military eyes-front position, she continued, "we're so close, just not quite there, Sergeant."

"You know DNA testing takes a long time. Why are you in such a rush?" He slightly relaxed his stiff posture, letting her know she was now on safer ground.

Caitlin blew out a breath and considered his question, "I hadn't really thought about it until now, Sergeant. Maybe it's because Fraser has destroyed the Sinclair family. I just want to give them some closure, boss."

"You aren't hunting Fraser. He's dead. You're searching for his killer," Williams folded his arms across his chest.

"Yes, boss, and yet in my mind, if I can tie this up, I'm honoring Lorna and Camden Sinclair," she said.

"And perhaps the Sinclairs are overjoyed that Fraser was murdered."

"They might be," Caitlin smiled tightly. "Am I wrong to want to resolve this quickly, Sergeant?"

"No, you're not wrong. You are a compassionate cop, Caitlin, and a skilled detective," Williams said. "Do it right, and don't let this one get under your skin."

"I understand."

"Organize your evidence. Decide what you want Detective McHugh to ask Mitchell Ross, then call him," Williams ordered. "Dismissed corporal."

"Yes, boss."

Jones gave Caitlin an exaggerated visual inspection as she re-entered their workspace. "You still seem to have all your body parts. I guess Sarge didn't chew your ass or bite your head off," he whispered.

Ignoring his teasing, Caitlin plopped into her chair. She did have vacation days owed to her. However, mortgage payments, home owner association fees, and property taxes emptied her bank account every month. She didn't have a surplus of cash to fund her absurd and short-lived rebellion. Creating a new document on the computer, she started listing what they knew and didn't know about the murder of Fraser.

"What are you working on now?"

Crushed

"As Sarge ordered, listing our evidence, and our questions for Ross, before I contact Detective McHugh in Toronto."

"What do you have so far?"

"Here's what we know. Ross rented a white Jeep for five days," she said, reading the bullet points of the document. "He returned it sooner than expected. He washed it before returning it. Human tissue was found in the suspension. The tissue has been sent for DNA analysis. We are waiting for the results. Ross attended the same high school as Lorna. He also attended the same university as both James and Lorna Sinclair. Sinclair found a photo dated 2007 of Lorna and Ross. Camden Sinclair was born in 2008. Ross attended the celebration of life but departed quickly when Sparky and Jessica exhibited an interest in him. He abandoned his paid return flight for a more expensive one-way ticket on an earlier flight." She met Jones' eye. "What else?"

"Flesh it out more," Jones replied, "so that McHugh will better understand our suspect."

"I will, and then this is my list of what we don't know yet. Why did Mitchell Ross wash the truck before returning it?" she asked. "I'm sure he was attempting to destroy the evidence, but I want to know his explanation."

"And we want to know why he suddenly left the funeral home and then paid a lot of money to change his flight."

"We also need his version of how well he knew Lorna Sinclair. And if Camden is his daughter." Caitlin banged her hand on the desk, "dammit! This is ridiculous. I want to be in that interview room."

"I agree, but that's not going to happen unless we get a positive identification of the DNA," Jones said. "I'm curious. How will you explain to the Toronto detective why Sparky was sniffing mourners at the celebration of life?" The right side of his mouth twisted in a mocking half-grin.

Caitlin turned, glared at her partner, and displayed her usual response to his teasing—a middle-finger salute.

"Classy."

"That's me, one hundred percent classy."

Chapter 40

Penticton RCMP Station

"Corporal Smith, this is Detective Callum McHugh from Toronto Police Service," a low-pitched voice rumbled in her ear when Caitlin answered the phone.

"Good afternoon, Detective McHugh," Caitlin said. "How's the weather out your way?"

Jones caught her eye and mouthed "Toronto?" when he heard her say, Detective McHugh. She nodded.

"Frigid! Snow is forecast for later this afternoon."

"Isn't that too early for snow?"

"We usually get a few days of light snow before the serious storms in December," he said.

"Hopefully, you won't get a big dump today," she said. "I assume you didn't call just to give us a weather update."

"No, I formally interviewed Mitchell Ross late yesterday."

"And how did that go?"

"Not the outcome that I hoped for," he said.

"Detective McHugh, I'm going to put you on speaker so that my partner Cst. Ethan Jones can join the conversation."

"Sure, and please call me Callum."

"Okay, Callum, you're on the speaker. Did you get the usual no comment or under the advice of my lawyer...blah, blah, blah, answer to everything?" she asked.

"Not exactly," McHugh's voice boomed through the speaker. "Mitchell Ross admitted that he had been Lorna's lover when they were young, and he told us that he left the celebration of life immediately afterward because he was overwhelmed with grief."

"He didn't leave immediately," she countered. "He was off to one side watching the crowd until he saw me walking in his direction," she said, purposely omitting any mention of Sparky and his sudden interest in Ross.

"Are you that scary?" McHugh asked.

"Nope, I'm a sweetheart. Just ask my partner."

"She's terrifying," Jones rebutted.

McHugh laughed lightly. "As for why Ross was in the Okanagan when Fraser was killed, he said he was drumming up new business for his firm."

"Do you believe him?"

"If you hadn't witnessed his sudden departure from the funeral home, his reason would have been credible, but...."

"You have doubts about the rest of his statement," Caitlin prompted.

"He owns an international marketing company based in Toronto, so looking for business in Penticton, in my opinion, wasn't a believable reason," he said.

"Did you ask for proof? A list of people he contacted?" Caitlin asked.

"Yes, and he said he would have his executive assistant email the information to me this morning," McHugh said. "Then, when I told him that tissue and several hairs had been found underneath the Jeep that he had rented, his face became so white I thought he might pass out. He denied everything, of course, and stammered out a lame excuse that a previous driver had probably hit a deer."

Jones leaned closer to the speaker. "Does he know that we don't have a positive DNA identification yet?"

"His lawyer immediately asked the question. I said it was at the lab with a priority rush on the results," McHugh explained. "I didn't fool anyone, least of all the lawyer. He knows the results can take weeks or sometimes months. Still, it rattled

Crushed

Mitchell Ross that the FIS technicians had found evidence that could potentially convict him."

"As I mentioned in my email summary, Ross washed the truck at least once that we know of before returning it to Avis," Caitlin said. "We are currently searching for coin-operated car washes between Keremeos and Richmond, hoping that he was captured on video cleaning the vehicle after the murder of Fraser. Once is borderline believable. Two or three washes, in my opinion, says he's guilty."

"I agree with you on that. However, at this point, it will be a waste of your time," McHugh replied. Caitlin heard him suck in a long breath, then exhale.

"What aren't you telling us?" she asked.

"Mitchell Ross committed suicide last night."

"Ah, bloody hell. Are you absolutely sure it was suicide?" she asked. "Could it have been a business deal gone bad? Or revenge because someone knew that Ross had killed Fraser?" Her brain hummed with alternate scenarios.

"No, I'm positive it was suicide. I've just emailed you a copy of his letter. It was handwritten and his ex-wife has confirmed it is his handwriting."

"Handwritten," she repeated, then added. "We both know that faking a signature is possible, but faking an entire letter is very difficult. Give me a minute to read it," Caitlin said, then opened the

Crushed

email and read aloud so that Jones could hear. "I killed Alan Fraser on Monday, November 21st, in Olalla, B.C. I had only intended to stash a large amount of drugs at his home and then phone in an anonymous tip. I was worried that he wouldn't be convicted for killing my biological daughter Camden Sinclair and I wanted to ensure that he received a long prison sentence," she said, nodding in agreement with the statement.

"I guessed that correctly. Camden was his daughter," Caitlin said, then continued reading aloud. "When I saw Fraser, my grief overcame me, and I ran him down. I just can't face dragging my son, Jackson, through a messy trial, and I can't face the prospect of life in prison. I am so very sorry for the terrible mess that I have created. And I sincerely apologize to my housekeeper Marta, as she will likely be the one who finds my body. Signed, Robert Mitchell Ross.'"

"Do you know who found him?" Jones asked. "I hope it wasn't his son."

"No, he is recently divorced and lives, or I should say lived, on his own in a downtown condo," McHugh answered. "He was right, his housekeeper, Marta Fuentes, found him this morning."

"Poor woman."

"Agreed," McHugh said. "We've referred her to victims' services for assistance. According to Mrs. Fuentes, Ross had been depressed since his wife left him."

"In his letter, Ross mentions his son. How old is he?" Caitlin asked.

"Jackson is about the same age as Sinclair's son Tyler," McHugh said.

"Suicide is an unsatisfying solution for our case," Caitlin said.

"Yes, it is," McHugh agreed.

"His letter doesn't sound very remorseful," Jones interjected.

Caitlin reread the words. "You're right. He makes it sound like he hit Fraser once, then left, not deliberately ran him over several times, and at some point, in his rampage, got out of the truck to ensure that Fraser was well and truly dead."

"Which the prosecutor could argue wasn't an uncontrollable moment of rage, but a cold-blooded killing and subject to a life sentence," Jones said. "And that might have contributed to his decision to kill himself."

"Good point, but still, suicide is a drastic solution," Caitlin agreed.

"How did he kill himself?" Jones asked.

"Overdosed. Unusual for a man, but not surprising since he confessed to buying a substantial amount of Fentanyl and cocaine," McHugh said.

Suicide statistics were well documented. Women typically overdosed on drugs combined with alcohol or slit their veins in a hot bath, while men favored hanging or a single-vehicle accident. Suicide by shotgun or rifle was less common because only twenty-five percent of Canadians possessed long guns. Suicide by handgun was the least common method, with only twelve percent of Canadians owning pistols.

"Well, thanks, Callum, for handling this. As you said, it's not the expected outcome."

"No problem. Call if you need anything else."

"Likewise. Thanks again." She said, and disconnected the call.

Chapter 41

Penticton RCMP Station

"What a damn mess. Two families shattered. Three if you count Fraser's mother." Caitlin wiped the whiteboard clean, erasing the record of their past inquiries and future lines of investigation of Alan Fraser, Lorna and Camden Sinclair, and Mitchell Ross. Both cases were closed and in her view, unsatisfactorily resolved.

"Fraser's mother wasn't too concerned that he'd been killed," Jones said. He busied himself with stacking evidence files in three separate document boxes destined for the storage vault. Each box was labeled with the date, case number, and name. Dry details of lives cut short.

"Yeah, you're right. The officer doing the next of kin notification said her only question was, did Alan have anything of value that she'd inherit." Caitlin replied. "I assume she'll inherit his farm, such as it is."

"I doubt there will be anything to inherit. I read in the online news that Nathan Lapointe's widow, Heather Lapointe, is suing Fraser's estate," Jones said. "Remember the ambulance that arrived at the hospital just after we interviewed Fraser? That was Lapointe. He died while being transported from Naramata."

"Yes, I remember," Caitlin said. "I'm no expert on real estate values, but a small farm, in a remote community, with a ramshackle house wouldn't be worth much. Even including the value of the few scrawny cows that I saw grazing on stubble, it's probably not enough to cover the legal costs of a court case."

"Then maybe Heather Lapointe will try to sue the trucking company that Fraser worked for," Jones speculated.

"I don't think she'd have any luck with that," Caitlin said. "Fraser was an independent. He worked for anyone who needed a truck and driver."

"What a sad mess," Jones dropped his gaze to the floor. An unrelated thought pushed into his thoughts, and without realizing he spoke it out loud, "I wonder what Fraser's life was like as a kid?"

Perplexed, Caitlin silently watched her partner. These last few days, he seemed blue, despondent at times. It was time to loosen his tongue with an adult beverage or two. She opened her mouth to ask him out for a celebratory drink when he interrupted her.

"I'll do the final paperwork first thing in the morning. But in the meantime, do you want to get a drink before we head home?"

"You read my mind," she chinned in Natalie's direction, "should we include the youngster? She did an amazing job on research, again."

Jones smiled and raised his voice to carry across the room. "Hey, pipsqueak, we are going for a drink at the Barking Parrot. You want to go out with us old folks?"

"Sorry, Mom and Dad, no can do. I have a date."

"With a real person?" he shot back.

"His profile says he's a real person. His name is Liam Hemsworth," Natalie said.

"Liam Hemsworth, the famous actor from the Hunger Games?" Jones asked.

"Oh, so that's why his name was familiar," Natalie replied coyly as she walked toward them.

"Seriously, Nat, who are you going out with?"

"A guy I've known since elementary school. He works in Vancouver, but he's home for a visit with his folks. I ran into him when I was leaving for work this morning."

"Ran into him? Not the best description, given the case we're working on," Jones replied.

"God no," Natalie agreed, "I should've said I bumped into him in the driveway at my parents' house."

Jones made a face. "Umm, that's not much better."

"Is he cute?" Caitlin asked, steering the conversation away from vehicular homicide.

"Yes, very. And fun to be with."

"Well, you kids enjoy your evening. We are going to celebrate the conclusion of the Sinclair-Fraser case."

"What? You didn't tell me."

"Just did," Caitlin said. "Robert Mitchell Ross confessed to killing Fraser and then overdosed last night."

Natalie's face registered surprise. "That's unexpected," she said.

"The confession or the suicide?"

"Both. I mean, we thought he was guilty, but we hadn't nailed the evidence yet."

"Nope, but according to his note, he was terrified of spending time in prison and didn't want to drag his teenage son through a messy court case."

"Huh," Natalie said. "Well, you old dears have a nice cup of tea and get yourselves off the bed at a decent hour."

"Watch your mouth, young lady. We'll have you reassigned to patrol," Caitlin threatened.

Settled in a quiet corner at the Barking Parrot with their beverages, Caitlin tipped her glass towards Jones. "To another case solved."

Jones clinked his glass lightly against hers. "Solved by the Dream Team."

"How do you figure that? Our suspect confessed."

"We had him on the ropes," Jones objected. "I think he knew the DNA evidence would convict him. He capitulated quickly once Detective McHugh told him the techs had found bits of tissue under the vehicle."

"True, but he confessed without knowing for certain."

"We would have nailed down the case in a few more days," Jones said.

"Okay, I'll give you that one. Does our Dream Team include Sparky?"

"Sure, but I'm starting to get flak from the others that we can't solve cases without that mutt."

Caitlin sputtered a laugh, "remember what I told you about the two Cancún detectives who were nicknamed Paw Patrol?"

"Don't mention that again," Jones mimed, zipping his mouth,

"You could always put in for a transfer to get away from Jessica and Sparky," Caitlin teased. "Someplace in the far frozen north."

"God, no! I don't want to be that cold, and besides, I like working at this detachment."

"Me too," Caitlin lightly punched his shoulder. "And I like working with you, *pardner*," she drawled.

"Same here."

"So, what's going on with you, Ethan?"

A shutter dropped over his face, and his laughter died. "What do you mean?"

"You've been unhappy for a few days now," Caitlin watched his face collapse as he blinked back tears.

He fidgeted with his glass making a series of wet circles on the table and avoided her gaze.

"Did you and Meaghan have a tiff?"

"No, it's Rowan. He's sick."

Caitlin placed a comforting hand on his forearm. "Tell me."

"The doctor says he's not absorbing the nutrients from his food, properly. I really don't understand. We give him the best of everything and we love him so much."

"Have the doctors done tests?"

"Yes, we've taken him to the hospital several times for tests. Meaghan is devastated. She's researched and read everything, trying to figure out what we are doing wrong," Jones said. "It's why I wasn't interested in flying to Toronto to interview Ross. I was worried that something terrible would happen while I was away."

"Cross that one off your worry list. We won't be flying to Toronto," Caitlin said. "I'm sure Rowan will be just fine. Some kids develop more slowly."

Jones lifted his red-rimmed eyes. "And you're the expert on childrearing?" His attempt to smile slipped sideways and disappeared.

"I listen when my cousins talk about their kids." She lifted one shoulder. "Sometimes. Occasionally. Honestly, hardly ever," she admitted. "I'm the fun cousin who arrives once a year with loads of gifts and forbidden candy."

Ignoring her attempt to make him laugh, he whispered, "Doc Liz once told me she never wanted to meet Rowan...in her office."

Chills ran down Caitlin's spine. *Her office: the morgue.* "He'll be okay, Ethan. Kids are tough." She gave his arm a reassuring squeeze. "Come on, partner, you should go home and give your beautiful wife a kiss and your handsome son a hug."

Jones nodded, drained his glass, and shrugged into his jacket.

"Let's hope we both get some sleep tonight," Caitlin said. "Tomorrow, I have to update James Sinclair and tell him the case is closed."

Chapter 42

Summerland

Caitlin parked the unmarked police car in the driveway at the Sinclair home. From the outside the home looked the same—a happy place for a happy family—while inside the heartbreak continued.

Once again, she rang the doorbell, and lifted her chin so that she was visible through the door cam.

Sinclair opened the door with a puzzled expression. "Yes?" he asked.

"Good morning, Mr. Sinclair. May I come in?"

"All right," he said, standing back and opening the door wider. "Were we expecting you?"

"No, sir, you weren't." She followed Sinclair into the kitchen, noting he took a moment to lock the door again, barring his intrusive neighbor. In the living room his blankets and pillow were still stacked on the end of the couch, but overall, the main level looked tidier and smelled cleaner.

"Please have a seat. Would you like a coffee?" he asked.

Caitlin sensed from his lackluster demeanor that his offer of coffee was automatic and not sincere. "No thank you sir, I've just had a coffee."

Sinclair pulled out a chair and sat down. "Is there something new in the case?"

"Yes, sir." She had spent an hour with Sarge, working out a legal and ethical way to tell Sinclair about Mitchell Ross. If the Crown Council had charged Ross, the information would have been available to the public. But, because the charges were pending when he confessed, it was a gray area. She sincerely hoped she didn't make a mess of it.

"Is Tyler at home?" she asked.

"No, he is at his friend's home. Playing video games."

"It's good for him to be with his friends," Caitlin said. She was thankful Tyler wouldn't inadvertently overhear the conversation. Sinclair could decide later how much he wanted his son to know.

"Do you remember the photo that you gave me? The one of Lorna and a man named Mitchell?" she asked.

"Yes, of course I do."

"His full name is Robert Mitchell Ross. Does that name mean anything to you, sir?" she asked.

"Rob Ross? I have been ransacking my memory, searching for a man named Mitchell, but I couldn't think of anyone by that name. Rob Ross and Lorna were friends at UBC, and, I think they shared one or two classes. I only met him a couple of times, and didn't recognize him in the photo," Fraser answered. "What does he have to do with the case?"

There is no easy way to tell Sinclair the truth. She looked him in the eye, and said, "Mr. Ross has confessed to killing Alan Fraser, the truck driver that ran into your wife and daughter. With his confession the cases are closed."

"That makes no sense." Fraser's face registered his confusion. "Why would Rob murder Fraser?"

"Mr. Ross claims to be Camden's biological father," she said.

"What?" Sinclair stared at her. "Did you just say he claims he is Camden's real father?"

"That's what he stated in his signed confession."

"He's a liar!" Sinclair shouted. "Lorna wouldn't cheat on me."

Caitlin kept quiet. When Sinclair had handed her the photo he had accused Lorna of doing exactly that, of having an affair with the unfamiliar man. Sinclair was suffering and she didn't need to remind him of his angry allegations.

"I want to talk to Ross. To set him straight," he demanded.

"I'm afraid that isn't possible, Mr. Sinclair," Caitlin said. "Mr. Ross committed suicide."

"No!" Sinclair shouted. "He makes a preposterous claim, then kills himself, not giving me the opportunity to prove him wrong! That's bloody unbelievable." Sinclair stared at her. "That's not right," he whispered. "It's just not right."

Caitlin reached out her hand and laid it on his forearm. "I'm so sorry Mr. Sinclair."

Chapter 43

On the Edge Winery

Mike opened the front door and shouted, "Jess! Come here. I've bought you a present."

The frenzy of the harvest was over, the grapes had been pressed, and the juice, securely stored in fermentation tanks, was slowly aging into a new vintage. Life had slowed again to a comfortable pace as the weather fluctuated between late fall and early winter temperatures. The nights were longer and the days shorter with Christmas only five weeks away.

Joining Mike in the driveway Jessica shivered in her light jacket. The bright sunshine had fooled her. The temperature was colder than she thought it would be.

"What is this?" she asked, running her hand over the worn, pale gray paint on the fender of the old car. The outline of the front fenders reminded her of a shapely eyebrow, swooping to a smooth peak at the beginning and dropping away to a finer point at the bottom. She noticed the black top was folded behind the seats. One thing she did know, it was a convertible. An ancient convertible.

"A 1948 MGTC," Mike answered. His pleased grin bunched his cheek muscles and accentuated the laugh lines in the corners of his eyes.

"Why?"

"Why what?"

"Why did you buy it?

"You wanted a convertible."

"Yes, I did, and thank you for thinking of me." Jessica slowly nodded her head, wondering why he didn't understand the irrationality of his purchase. "However, I wanted a convertible for the summer, not November, and this is a right-hand drive, built for British roads, not for North America," she said, pointing at the long gearshift shaft on the left side of the driver's seat.

"The MGTC was only ever built as a right-hand drive," he answered matter-of-factly. In his mind it was a logical explanation.

"I don't know how to shift with my left hand. Can you teach me?" she asked. She might as well be a good sport about the situation.

Mike shrugged lightly, "I'm just learning myself."

"Then we can both learn to grind the gears."

"It would be better if we didn't mash the gearbox too much." He gave her a sheepish smile. "It is seventy-odd years old, after all, and

Crushed

synchromesh hadn't been invented when this baby was built," he said, gently patting the antique vehicle.

"Got it," she opened the door, dropped behind the steering wheel, then reached down, searching for a lever to pull the seat forward. "How do I adjust the seat? I can't reach the pedals."

Mike rubbed a hand over his shiny dome and grinned. "Yeah, well, that takes a bit of work with a wrench."

"So, if I adjust the seat for me, then we have to re-adjust it for you?"

"Yep, that's about it," he agreed, quickly changing the subject. "As you can see, she needs a paint job. What color would you like?"

Puzzled about the non-adjustable seat problem, Jessica recognized Mike's change of subject for what it was, deflection, and went along with his ploy. "Blue. It's my favorite."

Mike made a face, then gave her a little regretful shake of his head. "I'm sorry, sweetie, that's not a stock color for 1948."

"British Racing green?" she offered a guess, even though the idea of a green car didn't thrill her.

"No, it's not stock either."

Jessica rested both hands on the steering wheel and turned the full force of her blue eyes on

Mike, "then what color should I pick?" she asked crisply.

"Red. Regency Red."

"That's a great idea, Mike. Why don't you have the car painted red?"

"Sure, red it is!" He answered, deliberately ignoring her sarcasm.

Jessica pulled herself out of the car and carefully closed the driver's door. "I'm going to spend some time today and find an inexpensive everyday car."

Mike nodded distractedly as he slid into the car. "Yep, good idea. I'll drop you off on my way to the body shop."

"Body shop?"

"I made an appointment to take this little beauty in for new paint and upholstery," he said. "I just wanted you to see her first."

Jessica bit down on the retort that sat on the tip of her tongue, begging to be asked. *What happened to staying within our budget? To cutting back on expenses?*

They had been living together for two years with no long-term plans, which suited her just fine. His money was his, and hers was hers. But, to be fair, Mike earned more money than she did, and he happily contributed extra to their living expenses.

Crushed

It wasn't her job to regulate his spending. But... *just stop it, Jessica.*

Eyeing the instrument panel as he started the car, Mike asked. "Are you ready to go? The appointment is for ten o'clock."

"And how are you planning to get back to the winery?"

"Lauren is in town picking up supplies with the company truck. She said to call her when I was ready." Mike replied, his hands caressing the steering wheel.

Annoyed, she chewed the inside of her cheek. *Lauren knew about the car before he mentioned it to me.* "You go ahead. I need to walk Sparky," she said.

Sensing a change in her mood, Mike tipped his gaze up. "Everything okay, Jess?"

"Yep. Peachy. I'll catch you later." Feeling obstinate and uncooperative, she went inside the cottage, where she watched Mike happily drive off in his new toy. Damn, she loved that guy, but at times, he was a colossal pain in the proverbial butt. Preaching economy and practicing indulgence.

"A present for me, my ass! Even Lauren knew about the car before I did," she huffed and looked down at Sparky, who was cautiously eyeing her, waiting for a further explosion of cusswords. "You know me too well, pooch. Let's take a walk.

I'll look for a useful vehicle another day—when I calm the hell down!"

She shrugged on a warmer jacket, stuffed gloves, and a hat into her pocket, and strode outside. Sparky scooted ahead.

While Jessica fiddled in the kitchen, organizing cheese and crackers to accompany their evening glass of wine, Mike pointed the remote at the television and increased the volume of the song playing through the Stingray Music app.

"I love that song!" Jessica shouted over the music.

"Dance with me, beautiful?" Mike asked, holding out his hand.

"Sure!" She closed the fridge door and danced from their kitchen to the living area. Mike grabbed her hand and twirled her into a rock-and-roll jive with a few two-stepping cowboy moves.

"I miss dancing in the moonlight on the beach," she said wistfully.

"How about the time that we danced out the door of Javi's Cantina and down Juarez Avenue?"

Laughing, Jessica let herself be spun into and back out of Mike's embrace. "That was hilarious."

Crushed

"And Javi posted it on their Facebook page."

"I remember. It was such a fun night."

He gently drew her close to his chest. "Are you over being mad at me about the car?" He smiled into her eyes.

Jessica grinned. "How did you know I was annoyed?"

"I have my ways." He gave her a slow sexy kiss.

When their lips separated, she continued their earlier discussion. "But why buy a standard car with a left-hand shifter? And seats that don't adjust without using a wrench?"

"You know I'm a car nut." He spun her away, then back.

"Doesn't answer my question."

"Years ago, I rented a car in Britain. At that time, automatics were rare in Britain or even in Europe, so I had to drive a standard and discovered I sucked at shifting with my left hand. After two days, I gave up and took the car back." He shrugged. "And that's always bugged me." He wrapped his arms around her and laid another sensual kiss on her mouth.

"Are you trying to rewrite your youth?" she teased.

He shrugged again. "Not rewriting, let's say, fixing a minor annoyance."

"And speaking of annoyances," she said, her eyes snapping with irritation.

And...we are not done yet. He intently watched her face, wanting Jessica to believe he was taking her concerns seriously. He bit the inside of his cheek so he wouldn't laugh and accidentally ignite a fiercer tirade. Nothing annoyed a partner more than laughing at their concerns.

"I did a little research on the MGTCs. And in 1948, they introduced a new color combination. Ivory and Clipper Blue. So, we could have the car painted blue even though you said, that's not a stock color for 1948."

Mike struggled, but he couldn't contain his laughter. "Okay, you got me," he sputtered. "But the shop had already ordered the paint, and it was too late to change my mind about the color."

"So, we have a car that you purportedly bought for me, that is going to be red, my second least favorite color for a car next to green, and it is a left-hand shift, with seats that won't adjust for my shorter legs."

"True. But you love me."

She laughed and kissed him passionately, "God help me. I do love you."

Crushed

"Do you love me more than Sparky?" he asked for the second time in a few days.

"Maybe."

"Do you love me enough to marry me?" He pulled a glittering diamond ring out of his pocket and held it up for her to see.

The End

Acknowledgments

Writing is a solitary obsession with hours spent creating, considering, and correcting.

However, I have had assistance from some amazing friends whom I have reconnected with since returning to Canada:

- Mary Fry, owner of Mary Fry Designs, for the cover design
- Eric Von Krosigk, wine consultant, the winemaker at Frind Estate Winery, West Kelowna, and a good friend.
- The fun and helpful folks at the Ruby Blues Winery: Prudence Ruby Mahrer owner, Beat Mahrer, Kerry Younie, Sharon Hickey, and Melanie Haley
- Graham Pierce, winemaker Ruby Blues Winery
- Dave Prechel
- Sean Neary
- Kevin Fai, Runtime Computers & Design
- Manuscript proofreaders include Sue McDonald Lo, Janice Carlisle Rodgers, Kyla Daman-Willems, Kim Lawton, and John Arendt. I truly appreciate your continued patience with my random punctuation and helpful suggestions and corrections.

Any remaining errors are my responsibility.

There are three other groups of people I would like to thank for their continuing encouragement and support:

- Fans of my bilingual books for children; The Adventures of Thomas and Sparky;
- Fans of the Isla Mujeres Mystery series;
- Friends from Isla Mujeres and the Okanagan Valley who patiently answered my endless questions.

About the author

Born in a British Columbia, Canada, gold mining community that is now essentially a ghost town, Lynda has had a diverse, and some might say eccentric, working career. Her job history includes bank clerk, antique store owner, ambulance attendant, volunteer firefighter, SkyTrain transit control center supervisor, a partner in a bed and breakfast, a partner in a microbrewery, and hotel manager. The adventure and the experience were always more important than the paycheck.

Writing has always been in the background of her life, starting with travel articles for a local newspaper, an unpublished novel written before her fortieth birthday, and articles for a Canadian safety magazine.

When she and her husband, Lawrie Lock, retired to Isla Mujeres, Mexico, in 2008, they started a weekly blog, Notes from Paradise, to update friends and family on their newest adventure.

Needing something more to keep her active mind occupied, Lynda and island friend Diego Medina self-published two bilingual books for children, *The Adventures of Thomas the Cat / Las Aventuras de Tómas el Gato* plus *The Adventures of Thomas and Sparky / Las Aventuras de Tómas y Sparky*.

One thing led to another, and Lynda created and self-published the Isla Mujeres Mystery series, set on the island in the Caribbean Sea where they lived. Following the death of Lawrie in 2018, she and Sparky remained in Mexico until the COVID-19 pandemic became a reality.

In March 2020, Lynda and Sparky decided to return to the Okanagan Valley, Canada. The Death in the Vineyard series combines two things dear to her heart: Canada and good wine.

The legal stuff

The characters and events in this book are purely fictional except for the following:

Jessica Sanderson is a product of my imagination, but like me, she was born in Canada. She shares my off-beat sense of humor, potty mouth, and a love of critters;

Mike Lyons is a mix of my husband, Lawrie, and other treasured friends.

Carlos Mendoza shares Lawrie's good sense of humor, the love of dancing, and the appreciation of Rolex watches and expensive cars;

Yasmin Medina is fictitious, but she is tall with curly hair, like my friend Yazmin Aguirre;

The No Regrets Winery and Vineyards, On the Edge Winery and Vineyards, and Dream Chaser Winery, are fictitious; they are not based on any particular winery.

Any other resemblance to persons, whether living or dead, is strictly coincidental.

All rights reserved.

No part of this book may be reproduced or transmitted in any form by any means, electronic or mechanical, including photocopying, recording, scanning to a computer disk, or by any information storage and retrieval system, without written permission from the publisher.

Crushed
Published by Lynda L. Lock
Copyright 2023
Print Copy: ISBN 978-1777-2510-9-3
Electronic Book: ISBN 978-1777-2510-8-6

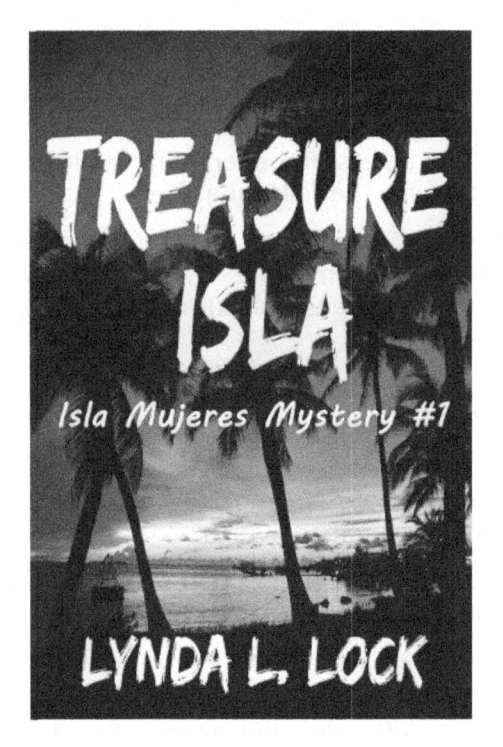

Treasure Isla Book #1

Treasure Isla is a humorous Caribbean adventure set on Isla Mujeres, a tiny island off the eastern coast of Mexico. Two twenty-something women find themselves in possession of a seemingly authentic treasure map, which leads them on a chaotic search for buried treasure while navigating the dangers of too much tequila, disreputable men, and a killer. And there is a dog, a lovable rescue mutt.

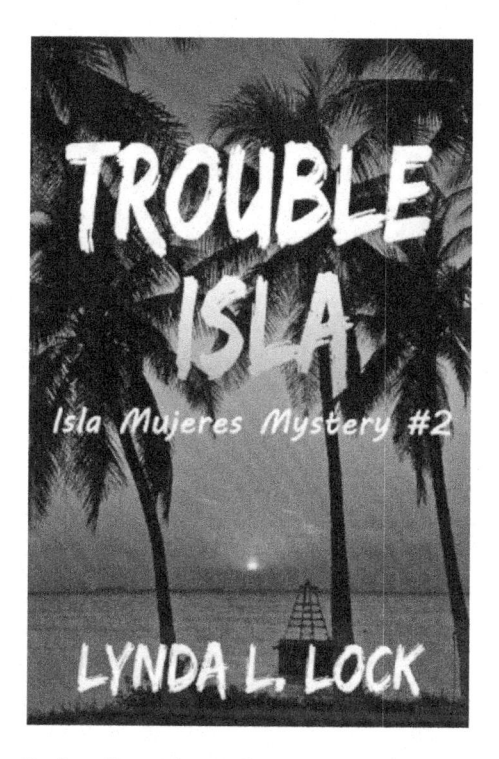

Trouble Isla Book #2

"This pair of leading ladies are fun to immerse in for an afternoon escape. The character development is richly layered and entertaining. The stakes are also enjoyably high, and the action sequences will keep readers voraciously flipping pages. Trouble Isla is a quick, unpredictable read. Bringing this small Caribbean Island to life and populating it with vivid characters that will continue to carry this series forward, Lynda L. Lock has created a uniquely colorful mystery." Self-Publishing Review, ★★★★

Tormenta Isla Book #3

A mysterious disappearance of a local man and the looming threat of multiple hurricanes headed toward the peaceful Caribbean Island of Isla Mujeres create havoc in the lives of Jessica, her friends, and her rescue mutt, Sparky.

Diego held up his smartphone and silently showed her the screen, pointing at the NOAA graphics.

Her eyes opened wide in surprise as she looked at the screen, then a frown crinkled her brow. "Really? Three hurricanes?"

"Si," he responded, "Pablo, Rebekah, y Sebastien."

Temptation Isla Book #4

Rafael Fernandez leaned forward, resting his elbows on the polished wood, tapping his fingertips together. "Take them all out! At the reception." He said, sweeping his right hand sideways as if knocking a pile of papers from his desk to the floor.

Alfonso paused momentarily, considering his next words. He had to get this precisely right, or at the very least, he would be demoted to the riskiest tasks or, in the worst-case scenario, killed for insubordination. Depending on Fernandez's mood, the flick of a finger or a chin pointed at a victim could quickly end that person's life.

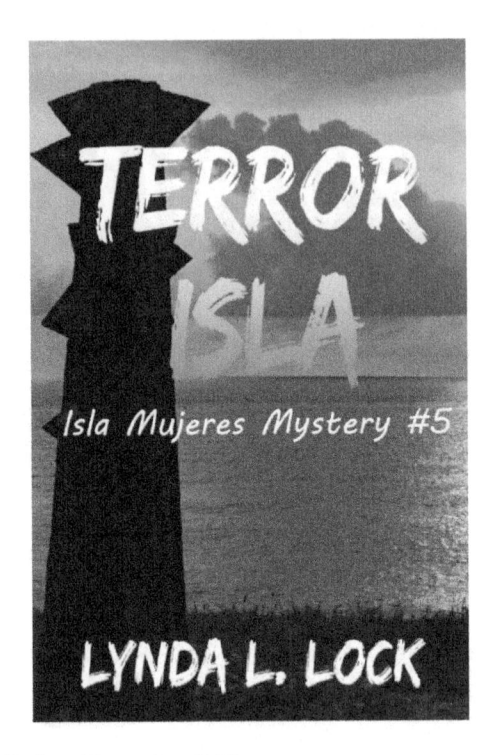

Terror Isla Book #5

Isla Mujeres, a tiny island paradise in the Caribbean Sea, is rocked by a power struggle between a Mexican cartel and a Romanian gang as they battle to control the illegitimate ATM skimming. Significant changes are coming for Carlos and Yasmin, while Jessica Sanderson fends off an angry lover from her past. Sparky, Jessica's stocky beach mutt, is once again at the center of another Sparky-situation.

"I want a superhero cape. A red one," Diego Avalos said. "I am feeling very underappreciated."

"In Jessica's opinion, Sparky is the superhero with the red cape. We're his minions doing his bidding," Pedro rejoined. "I'll pick you up in ten minutes."

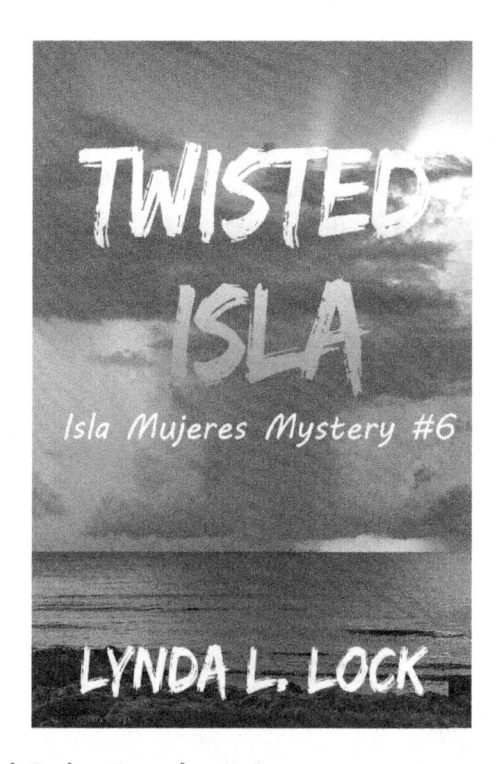

Twisted Isla Book #6

Death stalks the annual Island Time Music Festival. Nashville musicians and songwriters flock to the tropical island of Isla Mujeres to raise funds for the Little Yellow School House. Jessica and her keen-nosed beach-mutt Sparky are thrown into another murder mystery.

Sergeant Ramirez held up his palm with his fingers spread wide, "That's the fifth body."

"Really?" Mike lobbed a startled look at Jessica.

What are Jessica and Sparky involved in this time?

Corked Book #1 Death in the Vineyards

Love, lust, and loot in the affluent world of wine and wineries.

Corked is the newest murder mystery from the author of the exciting Isla Mujeres Mysteries. Murder follows Jessica Sanderson and her detective dog Sparky as they relocate from their Caribbean paradise in Mexico to Okanagan wine country in Canada.

On Isla Mujeres, significant changes are coming for Jessica's friends as the COVID-19 virus gains momentum. Leaving her beloved island Jessica follows her new love interest, Mike Lyons, into a new adventure.

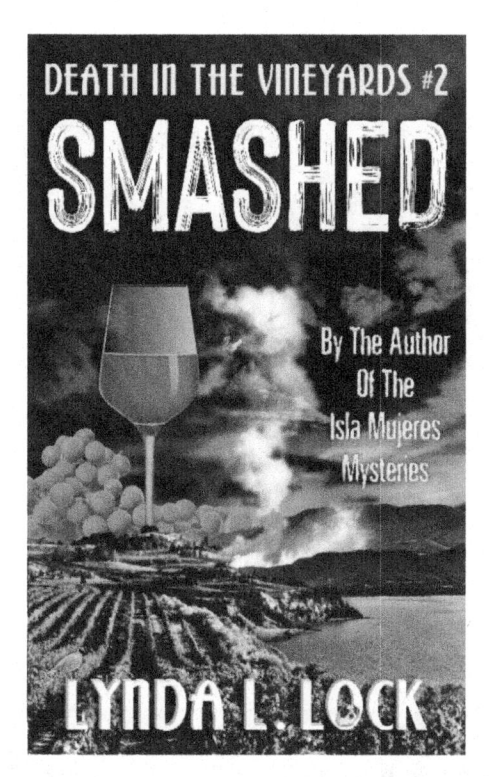

Smashed #2 Death in the Vineyards

Some people can convince themselves they can do no wrong.

While wildfires ravage the Okanagan Valley, Jessica Sanderson and her love interest Mike Lyons, battle to save two wineries; one from the massive wildfire threatening homes and businesses in Okanagan Falls and the other from economic disaster and the sudden death of their winemaker.

In *Smashed*, Jessica and her Mexi-mutt Sparky find themselves in a sticky situation. In this highly-anticipated sequel to *Corked*, inquisitive Jessica and Sparky's amazing nose are again meddling in a police investigation. Will the dynamic duo solve the crime?

Bilingual books for children

Crushed

Sparky and his writer

Made in United States
North Haven, CT
27 November 2024